Ardent Justice

Ardent Justice

Peter Taylor-Gooby

Matador
9 Priory Business Park,
Wistow Road, Kibworth Beauchamp,
Leicestershire. LE8 0RX
Tel: 0116 279 2299
Email: books@troubador.co.uk
Web: www.troubador.co.uk/matador
Twitter: @matadorbooks

ISBN 978 1785899 003
British Library Cataloguing in Publication Data.
A catalogue record for this book is available from the British Library.

Printed and bound in the UK by TJ International, Padstow, Cornwall
Typeset in 11pt Minion Pro by Troubador Publishing Ltd, Leicester, UK

Matador is an imprint of Troubador Publishing Ltd

To Sue

- and thanks to Diane Dane, David Ewens, James Essinger, David Pick, Peter Smith and many others who helped me with this book.

*Author's profits from this book will go to Shelter, the
housing and homelessness charity.*

Proudly supporting

Shelter

*Registered charity in England and Wales (263710) and in
Scotland (SC002327)*

1

Ade stared at the man seated in the executive chair in front of the picture window, bright sunlight all round him. She hated him. She hated all of them, the smooth self-confident brokers and traders in their smart business suits, the smell of the cologne they wore, the way they brushed everything she said aside, their casual sexism. She hated their world, the secretaries in the outer office, always women, always stick-thin, always eighteen, running their eyes down her clothes, their perfect lips sneering at her grooming, the paid help in the back office who manufactured the accounts for them, the clubs where they did all the deals – word of mouth old boy, nothing on paper, never anything on paper.

'My assessment stands,' she said.

He laughed as if they were sharing a joke. He took a silk handkerchief from his breast pocket and wiped it across his lips.

'Tax,' he said. 'Tax. Where would we be without our tax-inspectors? It's always a pleasure, young lady. But I agree nothing.'

'Please examine the spreadsheet.' She used her most formal voice but she was fumbling with the catch on the case of her lap-top. At last she got it open and swivelled it, so he could see the screen. 'I have estimated all transactions for the past month from your clients' records. You will see your estimated profits, your costs based on the standard model, and the tax liable.'

His eyes flicked to a briefcase, top quality, with two high security combination locks, lying at the corner of the desk furthest from her. Then he reached past it and picked up a sheet of paper covered in numbers.

'I see the Revenue has laptops now. Very modern.' He grinned as if amused. 'But I can't agree those figures. Here are my accounts, very different. Certified of course. I think my accountant should join our discussion. I'm sure she'll be able to explain everything. Thursday, 4.30? Then I could take you to dinner afterwards.'

'Mr Webster.'

'Call me Rex. I'll call you Adeline.'

'I cannot believe the rate of profit here is so low. You have some expensive art-work on your walls.'

She gestured towards the picture dominating the room, chalk on black paper, a massive helmsman in oil-skins at the wheel of a clipper under full sail fighting its way through towering waves.

'Tacita Dean, I think?'

He smiled at her.

'Your clients are wealthy. These offices are over £1700 a square metre.'

She glanced out of the window, across the river to the dome of the cathedral, the cross glittering in the bright sunlight, the office-blocks towering over it.

'You have a view.'

She hated all of them. They always delayed, always

produced a different assessment with costs that no one had ever thought of. Then you took the case before the Commissioners and you could see them sitting there, all men, all ex-business themselves, smiling and talking in their confident voices about their acquaintances, their schools, their clubs, about Monte Carlo and motor-racing and rugby.

'How do you think the health service is financed, Mr Webster? Pensions? The roads you drive your cars on? Aid for starving children?'

He grinned back at her and glanced at the photo in the leather frame on his desk, two smiling blond girls in identical school uniforms. 'My daughters. Like peas in a pod aren't they? Except that's the one with leukaemia. Or is it that one, I'm never sure?'

He chuckled.

'Only kidding. Yes. I go private anyway. Makes sense. The NHS is all bureaucracy, waste of money.'

You never had to sit there with your mother when she had the fall. You never had to wait for the ambulance. You never spent hours on the phone, pleading with the consultant's secretary for an appointment. Poor mother! The thing she worried most about that day was the mud on her cardigan. She kept picking at it. 'It doesn't wash dear,' she said as if she'd done something wrong. She never got to the top of the waiting list.

Ade slid the laptop into her briefcase and got up.

He held up his hand.

'It doesn't have to be like this, you know. Just hang on a moment.'

He reached for the briefcase on the desk, flipped it

open and extracted an envelope between two fingers. His eyes narrowed slightly as if he was calculating something.

'Why don't I give you this, just to help things along? A donation. Call it a Christmas present.'

An image of her fist smashing into that plump self-assured face filled her mind.

'Mr Webster!' she said, nearly stuttering. 'I can't believe what you're saying.'

He waved a hand.

'Never mind, just my joke. Only a Christmas card in there. Don't take it to heart.'

He reached down and slid the envelope into the briefcase, picked it up by the ends and held it forward. She took hold of the handle but he didn't release his grip.

'Or perhaps we could go for a drink? To show there are no hard feelings.'

He licked his lips. She stared hard at him and snatched back the case.

'Excuse me.' She turned to leave.

'See you Thursday, if not before,' he called after her. 'Don't forget.'

She stood waiting for the lift, striving to contain her anger, to mould it into something she could use. Workers from the other offices were gathering round her, all talking past her, across her, all of them ignoring her. They recognised her instantly. Revenue. One of the enemy on their territory. They were all so sleek, so well-dressed, so certain of themselves. She'd been part of that world once, when it all made sense.

The lift arrived and they crowded in front of her. A

slender young man with greased back hair pushed past her. 'I'm sorry,' she said, dipping her head. He ignored her.

'It's no crime to be clumsy,' her mother had said, and patted her hand. In this world it was. They judged you when you spilt your coffee in the coffee-shop, when you fumbled your change, when you bumped into someone in a queue.

When she got to the lift the doors were already closing in front of her. The sleek young man was standing beside them. He smiled at her. She saw he had his finger on the close button.

'Careful,' he said as the doors slammed shut. There was something in the tone of his voice, courteous, powerful, at ease with himself. That was how Colin had sounded talking to cab-drivers, waiters, flight attendants. She turned and pushed open the door to the stair-case and stood there. She felt chill and suddenly exhausted. Why was she doing this? The image of her mother when they got her on the stretcher flashed into her mind, her mother lying there, frightened, her eyes pleading for help. Then Colin and the way he compressed his lips when she asked him what he did in the new job, and he just said 'Spreadsheets. In the city.' Then she thought of Webster holding out the briefcase, his eyes on her as if he owned her, the same way he owned everything else he touched.

She gripped the rail and realised she still had her biro in her hand. She slipped it into her pocket and started down.

2

Ade sat back in her chair. She'd checked through all the calculations, all the algorithms and the modelling. She rubbed her hand across her eyes. She'd rewritten the assessment and added some references to precedents. Everything checked. She was right, she'd done everything the way Morwen had taught her, but they wouldn't pay. They never did. That's what broke Morwen's spirit in the end, though she never said.

She thought of Morwen and how they'd first met, two years ago. Ade wasn't a fast-streamer; you didn't get in the fast-stream when you did your degree part-time at Birkbeck. She knew she was as good as any of them, better than most, but she didn't have that slick style, that bland assurance they taught you at Eton and Oxford. Morwen didn't either, but she didn't care and Ade learnt that from her.

It was a bright spring day, her first day, and the wind had bustled her through the streets. She stepped out of the lift, her cheeks flushed, and there was Morwen: tall, nearly as tall as she was, with tightly curled black hair and dark earnest eyes, her hand held out in welcome.

'Good to see you! I'm Morwen Archer, your mentor. Let's get a coffee.'

So many coffees, so many hours spent together, with Morwen explaining her ideas and how to make them work. The method. It was all Morwen's work, although she gave Ade half the credit when they presented it to Denny.

It was simple really.

'Listen,' said Morwen. 'One in twenty businesses tells you their real profits – and those are the ones who've made a loss. No-one likes paying tax, so you pay your accountants and your profits shrink like an ice-cube in hot chocolate.'

Ade shrugged, her hand on the table, palm open.

'Where we go wrong is this: we try to work it out for each firm, look at their offices, the business they're in, how the market's going and so on. We make a guess, our best guess, and we negotiate. Downwards.'

Morwen's eyes sparkled.

'The big mistake is to treat each firm as separate.' She held up her fingers. 'One, two three, four, like this. But they're not just individual businesses, they're a network. They all do deals with each other. They provide services, consultancy, trade, transfers – you scratch my back, I scratch your back. That's how it works, that's why they're all here, next to each other, same office blocks, same clubs, same restaurants, all together in the city.'

'Yes,' said Ade, 'but how does that help?'

'Don't you see? They trade, the money goes round and round, they're all linked together.'

Morwen took Ade's hand and interlaced her fingers with hers.

'It's the same money. The profit of one is the business expense of another. So once we find out about one of them, we're tracing part of the network. Takes time, but we find out more and more, we get better at it.'

Ade kept her eyes on Morwen's face. Morwen continued: 'We catch one of them out and they have to pay a penalty, they don't like that. We talk to them, do a deal. They tell us the truth about who they trade with, what's really going on. We've got a bit more of the picture. We move on to the next one.'

She laid Ade's hand gently on the table.

'The city is a network and we can track all the links in our spreadsheets. Bit by bit and not tomorrow, but we'll do it, you and me.'

So Morwen and Ade, Ade and Morwen became a team. They trained others. They got noticed. They started to build up the Model, who was making the mega-profits, where the money was going, who should pay the tax. They became friends; they always seemed to be together, in the office, in the coffee-shop, visiting galleries, hanging out. Morwen loved art and she loved the exhibitions, all that London had to show. They became part of each other's lives.

The Model, that's what she'd had on the lap-top in Webster's office. Morwen's model. She'd do that for Morwen at least, just to show that someone remembered what she'd done. She sat there, thinking of Morwen, her solemn eyes, the smile on her face, the way she'd held Ade's hand, the way she looked at you when she was talking to you, as if you mattered more than anyone else in the world. She thought of how Morwen had looked the last time she'd seen her, in Bronzefield High Security Prison, with both hands pressed against the security glass as if she'd be able to touch Ade again and her face slumped forward as she whispered: 'You have to get me out of here, Ade. You have to get me out.'

Spend every night for a month on a case, she thought, that's what Morwen did. Check it and double check it, sitting here in an empty office, long after everyone else has gone. Put together a file, thick as a phone book, of evidence. Get it knocked back by some accountant you never even meet. Take it to the Commissioners and they look at you as if you're nothing, just an interruption to the important business, and they turn it down in a sentence. In the end Morwen couldn't take it. She cared about the job too much.

Ade opened a memo form on the laptop and typed:

'Re: R.Webster Consultancy.

Accounts not credible. Request refer to Investigations, full audit. Model attached.'

She tapped return. Somewhere behind her, at the other end of the office, the cleaners had started on the waste-bins.

She thought of Webster, of the expression on his face when he handed her the briefcase. She flipped open another memo form.

'Re: R.Webster Consultancy.

Request transfer alternative case, grounds of incompatibility.'

She sat there. Denny's decision. Denny would call her in to talk it over. She never decided anything without talking it through. Ade pressed return and closed the machine.

3

She sat there thinking of Morwen, her skin dark and glossy as a ripe aubergine, her eyes thoughtful, her lips always smiling. It was after she'd met Morwen that she'd known she was going to do something worthwhile. She remembered one time, fairly early on, when they'd been working on the Model all morning and it didn't balance and kept crashing and they'd missed lunch. In the end they'd gone for a coffee and they were at their favourite table in the window of the Gracechurch Street coffee-bar, just opposite the office.

Morwen took a bite out of her cup-cake and split the rest in half on the paper napkin.

'You never told me about yourself, why you're in the Revenue.' She nodded towards the main office. 'For most of them, it's a job. Except perhaps Jimmy the Kid; he's young, he thinks it's an adventure. But you're different.'

Ade nodded. She picked up half of Morwen's cake and put it carefully in her mouth. When she'd swallowed it she said: 'I think I'm like you, Morwen. Something touched me and I'm not going to let it go. This is how I make a difference.'

She fixed her eyes on Morwen's. She hadn't told anyone in the office about her family and she wasn't going to. When they asked her, she just said her parents were teachers. Well, she'd learnt a lot from them.

'My dad ran a betting shop. Numbers. That's where the spreadsheets come from, I guess. He always told me: "you've got to look after yourself in this world. No-one'll do it for you." He thought he was a sharp businessman. He wasn't much good at it, but when he had money he always gave me some. He wanted to do his best for me. So I spent the money on fees and books and worked and it got me through Birkbeck, just about.'

She broke her cake in half. Morwen picked up a piece and bit into it.

'Cherry and raisin, my favourite.' She licked the crumbs off her fingers. 'My Mum worked in a family centre. She always said we were the lucky ones. God put us here to look after anyone who was weak and vulnerable – frail elderly people, homeless people, families without anyone in a job – and that's what she did. She said the welfare state didn't come from heaven, it came because people cared and they paid for it.'

She ate the rest of her cake and neatly folded the napkin and dropped it into the paper cup.

'Yeah,' said Ade, 'that's the point. My Dad said you had to let other people look after themselves, but when Mum had her fall the waiting list was too long and there wasn't anyone to look after her. He kept saying he didn't understand it. He sort of gave up. When they took his shop, there was nothing for him. I tried to help but he said I should have my own life. One day, when I was at college, he took Mum's pills, all in one go, and that was that.'

Morwen squeezed her hand. 'I'm sorry.'

'Don't be. He couldn't even do that right. I called an ambulance and they pumped his stomach out. Now he's a frail old man and it's my turn to send him money.'

She was silent, staring down at her hands.

They sat there for a few moments, not talking, until Morwen said, 'Let's get some more cake.'

Ade watched Morwen as she went over to the counter and came back with two large cappuccinos, spilling the froth over the rims of the cups, and two pains-aux-raisin.

'I love those,' said Ade and smiled at her. Then she started crying, wiping her eyes with the back of her hand.

'It's OK,' said Morwen. She took Ade's hand and held it lightly in hers. After a while she started speaking again. 'I lied. My Mum never worked in a family centre and my Dad wasn't a social worker. Don't know who my Dad was. My Mum worked in a shop some of the time and sometimes in a pub, she wanted to do the best for me but she didn't know how.'

She paused, then continued: 'Didn't work out for me of course. She lost her flat and I was sent round various foster parents. I really missed her. She loved me and she wanted me back, but she couldn't cope with her own life and I knew the only person who'd look out for me was me.'

She'd stopped stroking Ade's hand. She gripped so tight it nearly hurt. Ade kept her eyes on Morwen's.

After a pause Morwen continued: 'So I made something of myself. I hate those bastards at the top who don't know what most people's lives are like, who can buy their way out of any problem, who shove past to get their snouts in the trough first. I decided I was going to make them pay some tax, so the rest of us can live decent lives and bring up our children, so there's social workers who've got time for you and decent housing and...' she smiled. 'But I'm going on. Actions speak louder. Let's get back.'

She picked up her coffee and led the way out of the café. Ade followed with her own drink and the two pains-aux-raisin in a napkin.

Later that day, in the pub after work, she told Morwen something else about herself: about Colin, with his spare, delicate face and his impossibly well-cut suits, how he'd seemed so bowled over by her, and how maybe he had been. For a month her life was a whirl of meals and pubs and the office and meetings and clubs and spreadsheets and weekends in Nice and Venice. He had taken her to the Adelphi and the Littleton and the Donmar and she had taken him to the Wallace and the Courtauld and the Tate and the RA and the National. Then he moved in and she felt her life was being lived on a larger scale, more splendidly. But something happened, she never knew what, and it all changed. He moved to the job in Canada Square that paid so well. He'd never say exactly what he did, but he seemed to work all the hours there were. One day he told her that he'd spoken to the senior partners and they'd said they could use her experience and they'd pay twice what she got in the Revenue. They had a blazing row and they both said things you can't take back. Then he was gone. No note, just a door-key on the mat.

4

The Model had been Morwen's big idea: a web of inter-linked spreadsheets where you put together all the fringe firms, the consultancies, the management experts, the risk advisors, the back offices, the outsourced accounting, the marketing people – all the specialist services that everyone seemed to buy in. After a while you began to see the patterns, the networks of ownership through intermediaries, the interest-free loans, the shared directorships, the exchanges of staff. Suddenly all the little micro-businesses, the ten person companies, the web-sites with nothing behind them but an office, a list of phone numbers and contacts with just the right people, didn't look so small. They all linked together like chain-mail. And you saw something else: how much money went out of the major players into the small fry, meaning they weren't really small fry after all.

The Revenue never bothered too much with the mini-businesses, not enough money there to make an investigation worthwhile, and if you do get something to stick, they just go bankrupt and start up under a different name somewhere else next week. When you saw the whole picture you realised how it all added together, and how city businessmen could buy a ten-million-pound town house as well as a place in the country. It explained why there was never enough tax coming in to finance a decent NHS or provide care for old people or keep the beggars off the streets or build housing that families could afford. And Webster wonders why I hate him.

A vacuum cleaner started up at the other end of the office. Ade looked round. Everyone else had gone. Time to make a move and get back to Whitechapel, but what was there to go home to? Images on a screen, something to eat and wine or gin. She should get an hour in the gym, but she always felt she was in the wrong place with all those lycra-clad bodies, everyone intent on their own programme. She needed a detox diet, she needed a personal trainer. Put it on the list.

She picked up her briefcase and remembered the laptop. She slid her hand down and felt something lying against it: a used brown A4 envelope, like a thousand others in city waste-bins that day. Webster. She opened it and stared at the card, a grinning Father Christmas with a sackful of money, and the wad of red-brown fifty-pound notes, the colour of the back of her father's hand, folded inside it. She felt the breath come fast in her throat. It was more money than she ever expected to see in one place in her life. A business expense, Webster would call it. She remembered the expression in his eyes when he held up the briefcase. He thinks he's bought me. I hate him.

I can't leave it here. If I spend it, he's got me. It's a test. So I give it to Denny first thing tomorrow morning. It'll be the police in the office, not a good career move. His word against mine. But nobody leaves that kind of money lying around. He's so damned certain of himself. Denny's OK, she did her best for Morwen.

She looked up. The safe was locked for the night. The cleaner glanced at her and turned her back. She closed the envelope and tucked it into her jacket pocket. *But what if I don't care? If I take the money and don't accept his figures? There's no-one else who knows about it, what's he going to go to the cops about? He accidentally left a wodge of cash in my brief-case?*

She was walking now, down the empty stair-well and out of the building, the wad of notes pressing against her chest. Her breath misted in the December air. She wrapped her overcoat tighter round her body. Office blocks rose up on either side, above the glow of the streetlights. She moved between pools of light and dark. *Is this how it felt for Colin when they made him the offer and he went over to the other side? "We'll triple your money, all you have to do is help us, tell us about your old friends. It's OK, no-one can touch you, none of it in writing."*

She kept her eyes ahead of her, staring down the street, south, across the river. On both sides shop-windows gleamed bright with Christmas displays. Giant crackers were strung across the street. They glowed amethyst, turquoise, crimson, the colours shifting, slowly merging into each other. Right in front of her stood a Christmas tree, the branches so dark that she only realised what it was from the outline in golden lights. Christmas, she thought. Happy Christmas, Mr Webster.

She heard a sudden rattle of detonations and a fountain of silver stars spurted up, soaring into the sky. She halted and gazed up at them. A rocket burst, a gigantic golden chrysanthemum, then another and another over the city. People were running past her, talking excitedly, jostling her. A nurse hurried by, swaying on high heels, then a figure lurched out of the shadows, one hand outstretched towards her. She backed away, her arms crossed over her chest. The streetlight shone down onto the vampire mask, picking out the fake blood dripping down his chin. An angel rattled a collection tin at her, smiling under the make-up. 'For the hospital.' She shook her head, then reached into her pocket and stuffed her change into the slot.

The students whirled on past her: a mummy in toilet-roll bandages, a giant teddy-bear, a space-alien. She walked slowly on, watching them as the clamour faded away. She took the usual short cut down Fish Hill past the Monument to the Great Fire. She always felt sad for it, dwarfed by the city blocks round it. She quickened her pace past a development site where the streetlights had gone out, and nearly tripped over a pair of legs in a grubby sleeping bag.

'Sorry,' someone grunted and the legs swung back into the shadow. She could make out a pinched face below a dirty woollen hat, both hands tugging at the bag.

'Sorry,' he said again, hunching down. He started coughing.

'No, my mistake.' She stood there. 'No problem.'

He looked helpless lying there. A thought crossed his mind.

'Any change?'

She felt in her pocket. It was empty. Across the river she could see the Shard and next to it the lesser office blocks. Webster and his gang were up there, she thought, they make this mess and they never have to come near the building sites, the dirty hidden places like this. She felt the dampness of the river in the air. She reached in her jacket and touched the envelope with the tips of her fingers.

It was a flat voice without accent. She stared down. He had brown eyes and long unkempt dark hair. His hands were still dragging the sleeping bag up to his throat.

The man stared up at her, then coughed and looked down. He didn't ask her again. She slipped a note out of the envelope. Why not?

'There you go.'

She placed it on the bag. He stared at it, then grabbed it.

'Christ, thanks miss, missis. I don't know, thanks,' he blurted out.

What should she say? "Have a nice one"; "Get yourself somewhere warm to sleep"; "Happy Christmas!"?

He was holding the note between both hands, staring at it. She could just make out the engraving in the dim light.

'Christ!' he said again.

She noticed movement in the shadows to her right. Someone was scrambling up out of a sleeping bag. She could hear voices in the darkness. Other figures were coming towards her. She backed away. She should go. The figure in the sleeping bag looked up at her. His eyes were soft, pleading. He started to pull himself out of the bag.

'Johnno!' said a voice, 'what's up?'

'She's only gone and give me a fifty!' the man said softly.

He'd got out of the bag now. He seemed like a giant

cuddly toy in his layers of jumper and anorak, newspaper poking out of the zip. She caught the smell of stale sweat.

He was right in front of her.

'I want to say thank you, miss.'

'I wanted to give it to you. Why shouldn't you have it?'

It seemed wrong to just walk away from him.

Someone touched her wrist. A woman with a thin lined face stood close to her, bundled up from head to toe, it seemed, in rags. 'Please miss. I got nothing.'

She looked round. There was movement everywhere, dark figures rising up towards her. She slipped another note out of her pocket and held it up. The woman released her wrist and reached out for the money. Ade swung round, but someone was blocking her way. There were others behind him.

She heard Johnno's voice: 'Take it easy. I can share.'

She stepped backwards and bumped against someone else. More people were moving out of the darkness. She had no idea there were so many of them, dark shapes wrapped in old coats and blankets and anoraks against the cold, their hands reaching out, coming towards her. She shrank back.

A slight figure slipped in front of the woman, seized Ade's arm and shouted: 'Come on!'

She was pulled forward and she was running alongside him up the steps and onto London Bridge. She turned her head and saw dark eyes, an unshaven face, skin the colour of milky coffee and chaotic black hair. Then they were in darkness. He stopped, breathing hard, and she stumbled to a halt and stood there, rubbing at her arm. She hated running, she'd never been any good at it.

'You're OK here. They won't come far.' He spoke gently

with no accent. 'They're not bad people, but they don't ever see money like that.'

'I'm sorry.' She felt awkward. 'I think he just wanted to say thank you.'

'That's Johnno – a big softy.' A smile passed across his face. 'But don't be sorry. Everyone always ignores you when you're on the streets, they just stare through you. It's something to be talked to like a human being.'

They were nearly over the river. A late train thundered over the rail bridge ahead of them.

'Maybe I could get you a meal?' she said.

He ate the all-night breakfast and extra bread, making little rushes at the food, then pausing, brushing the hair from his face and looking up at her with his sudden smile. So she told him about the money. For no reason at all.

He frowned then his brow cleared and the smile was back on his face.

'Robyn Hood,' he said. 'I like it. You're a bit of a character.'

'It's not like that, it just sort of happened.'

'That's what I mean. You didn't think about it, you just did it.'

He put down his knife and reached out to touch her hand, then thought better of it and took his hand back, his eyes timid. She found she was smiling at him.

The door of the café was flung open. Two policemen entered and stood on the threshold with the door held open, surveying the customers, cold air flowing in round them. No-one complained.

The taller of the policemen moved forward and

dropped a hand on her companion's shoulder. He tried to swing round but the hand pushed him into the chair.

'You. We've had complaints. You've been making trouble.'

She stared at the policeman; dark eyes and fleshy cheeks, red from the night air.

'Officer. He hasn't been doing anything, he's been here.'

The policeman glared at her. She saw where he'd trimmed his moustache unevenly above his lips.

'Not your business, miss.' He took in her suit, her smart coat, the briefcase. 'Best thing you can do is get home.'

'But he's my friend.'

'Word of advice. Be more careful about your friends, miss.'

The policeman pulled the black-haired man to his feet and glared down at him.

'OK you, you're coming with us.'

'But he hasn't finished his meal.'

'He's coming with us.'

The policeman squeezed the black-haired man's shoulder. Ade saw him wince. She looked up at him, her eyes shining.

'S'all right,' he said.

'But I don't even know your name.'

'Paul, Paul Affarn.'

He made a gentle gesture towards her with his free hand and the second policeman grabbed it. They hustled him to the door.

'Ade Corey, I'm Ade Corey,' she called out.

The door slammed shut, hard enough to make the glass rattle.

5

'Robin Hood, Robyn Hood.'

The rhythm of the late night train seemed to drum out the words. She gazed at the blackness outside the window, her double reflected back at her, its face staring into hers. Funny how everyone always assumed Robin Hood was a man's name. Paul was right: you don't have to be a man to take from the rich and give to the poor. She needed to think things through.

The flat was cold when she got back. She'd always felt it was cold since Colin had left. It was for the best. He'd been considerate enough to take his photo, everything that might remind her of him, or maybe it was selfish, maybe he had someone else to give them to.

Cup of tea, clean your teeth, bed. You need routines to get through things when you're by yourself. No routine and you find yourself waking up on the sofa and the TV screen's blank and the wine-bottle's empty and you're thinking that it's going to be a bad day tomorrow, except it's today and you're already late.

She lay there staring at the ceiling for a long time. When she slept it was to jumbled dreams: the moment when she found the envelope and all the different paths lay in front of her; Webster's face sneering at her; the homeless people, not really people but shapes coming up at her; and Paul, the warmth in his eyes, his quick nervous gestures. She woke up with a jerk.

'Next.'

Ade glanced round the dingy waiting room at the others bundled into their coats, all of them staring straight ahead, pretending Southwark Police Station wasn't the kind of place they ever came to normally, none of them smiling. No-one moved. She stepped up to the counter.

'I'm here to enquire about someone who was brought in last night.'

'Name?'

The desk sergeant tapped at the computer. She had vivid red lipstick and fair hair cropped short.

'Paul Affarn.'

'No, your name.'

'Oh, I'm Ade Corey.'

The sergeant typed her name carefully, read something on the screen, glanced at her and nodded. 'Mr Affarn. Yes, we know him. There was a bit of trouble and we had him in here last night, but there were no charges. City of London force wanted him for questioning, so they picked him up.'

'But what was it about?'

Ade became aware that the woman on her left had moved slightly and was listening to their conversation.

'Can't say. But,' the blue eyes stared at her, taking her in, 'Word of advice, Ms Corey. He's not the sort of person you want to associate with. A regular here, you might say. Occupy London. That peace camp at St Paul's. Aggravated trespass. Conspiracy. Incitement. That kind of thing.

Known to the City force too.' The sergeant looked away. 'Next.'

Ade walked over to the door. As she opened it, she glanced back. The desk-sergeant's eyes were fixed on her.

Silly idea going there, she thought as she walked on. There was movement at the end of a side alley, but she ignored it, there were people all round her, all going about their business. *No-one's going to recognise you, no-one's going to think you're someone with a pocketful of fifty-pound notes, no-one's going to help you. Why should they? There's no way you'll find him.* She stood there on Borough High Street, people pushing past her. A man in a smart overcoat said 'Excuse me,' clipping the words and shoving her aside. She turned onto Tooley Street then down a side road and found the café she'd taken him to last night, under the railway. He wasn't there.

'Never seen him before,' said the woman behind the bar. She looked down, running a cloth over a spotless counter. 'Don't want to, he bring the cops here.'

She left the café and walked on over the bridge towards King William Street with the Monument to the right. It was a crisp December day, early morning, and crowds of people were hurrying to work in the city, all of them wrapped up in themselves. Sunlight gleamed on the buildings across the river. She watched a tourist boat gliding past, all the faces turned up to stare at her. People were streaming over the bridge, huddled in quilted jackets or warm overcoats like hers.

She moved slowly on, down Monument Street and past the area where the rough sleepers had been. Now all she could see were a few pieces of torn cardboard. She thought she glimpsed someone against the sunlight, back by the Monument, staring at her, but she couldn't be sure. At an angle in the buildings, out of the wind, a figure in a hooded red anorak crouched on the pavement, a piece of cardboard in front of her with 'Don't Do Drugs, Please Help' written on it in biro. Ade stopped and looked down. A young woman, her face strikingly pale, stared back at her.

'Please,' she said.

Her arms were folded across her chest, her hands jammed under her armpits.

Ade walked on, felt in her pocket, turned and dropped a pound coin on the cardboard.

'Thank you.'

The woman spoke so softly that Ade could barely make out the words. She thought of Johnno last night, and the way he'd stared at the fifty-pound note.

'It's OK.'

Ade reached down and dropped another coin. A smile flashed across the young woman's face.

'Do you know someone called Paul?' Ade asked. 'Last night, he was here last night.'

'Don't remember none of it, there was a crazy woman with money. The cops came. I keep out of it.'

The girl hunched down further in her clothes. She couldn't be more than eighteen, Ade thought. She took out a five pound note and slipped it under the cardboard.

'There you go.'

She was on Gracechurch Street, the traffic fumes heavy in her throat. Two policemen in stab vests were coming towards her on the other side, wearing black gloves and black leather belts with radios, cameras and Tasers. One of them touched the other on the arm when they caught sight of her and they stood there staring at her. She hurried on. After thirty metres she looked back. No sign of them.

Never had any trouble with the law and suddenly there's cops looking at me like they know who I am. If it's me they're looking at. She thought of the day she came into the office first thing and Morwen was already there, still there from last night, her eyes glistening with enthusiasm. She hadn't slept, she'd finished the Model by herself.

She couldn't stop talking, Ade had never seen her so excited. Her fingers rattled across the keyboard. She'd made it all work, everything balanced, the nested spreadsheets, every single link. She'd already submitted it to the Chief Executive and the Minister's office, with copies sent to the Permanent Secretary and all the Board members. She had requested a formal investigation into all the major city consultancies. She wasn't going to wait while it went through the official channels and came back in a month's time with 'No Action Required' stamped across it.

'If this doesn't work, we'll leak it straight to the media,' she said. 'Ade, I know I'm right.'

Within two hours there were three cops, City of London, in stab-vests and carrying a warrant, hustling her out of the building. They'd sealed off the end of the office and taken her computer, everything from her desk. They refused to take statements from the other staff, telling them the case was not to be discussed. 'Signed the Official Secrets Act when you joined the Revenue, didn't you? This is an official secret.'

Then there'd been the trial, Ade remembered the headlines, all about state snoopers and industrial espionage and unauthorised data-gathering, with no details given on grounds of commercial confidentiality. The Revenue denied all knowledge of Morwen's work, Ade was never called, Morwen lied to protect her and Denny covered up. At least she did that for them. Morwen had cut a corner, just the tiniest corner, the last bit of data estimated and fitted in pat, to make it all work. Somehow they spotted it, and it was false accounting and fraud and extortion of legitimate profits and conspiracy with persons unknown and breach of trust in a public office – all requiring exemplary punishment. They must have had so many people on the case, combing through every detail. Then the news went through the office like a shockwave, that Morwen was taking the full blame herself and it was too late to do anything, and she was in Bronzefield and that visit was the last time Ade saw her.

She became aware of someone walking beside her.

'Hi.'

'Paul!' She stopped. 'What are you doing here?'

'Nothing much. They let me out.'

'I know – I went to the police station in Southwark. They said the City of London police wanted to question you.'

'You been looking out for me? I thought I was supposed to be looking out for you.'

'I wanted to thank you,' she said. 'For last night.'

'S'all right.' He rubbed at his left ear. 'I work on the streets these days, just making sure people are OK.'

He stepped closer to her. He was slightly shorter than she was. She could see tiny wrinkles round his eyes when he smiled.

'Just glad I was there,' he said.

'Me too.'

She said it before she thought. His shoulders were so thin under the jacket. He'd cleared the plate last night like he was half-starved. There was a kindness in his eyes; he gave you his full attention, the same way Morwen did.

He stood there smiling at her.

'Guess I should get to work,' she said after a while.

'Yeah, me too. 'He gave a half-wave, palm open. 'So long.'

'See you again.'

She turned but she hadn't taken half a dozen paces before he was there, walking beside her. 'Don't go,' he said softly. Then: 'Why do you think those cops were staring at you, back there?'

'I should be at work already. I'm glad you're OK.'

'City of London cops. Red and white hat-bands. You've got to be careful. Someone's keeping an eye on you.'

'Thanks.'

She touched his shoulder. His face lit up.

'Gotta go,' she said. 'See you.'

6

'What is your job, Adeline?'

The grey eyes were fixed on her. A woman Ade had never seen before sat behind Denny's desk, in Denny's chair. Her dull blonde hair was tied back too tightly, her lipstick too striking. She leaned forward, alert. Ade thought of a hunting dog. *With cheek-bones like those you're in the wrong job.*

Denny, Ade's line-manager was on an upright chair between the bookcase and the window. Denny with her round, comfortable face and smooth cheeks and brown eyes, she always reminded Ade of a country wife. You could trust Denny. The room was already in shadow at nine am. A blank brick wall rose immediately opposite the window. Denny smiled at Ade and nodded.

'I'm a tax-inspector, grade seven.'

'So what's your job?'

'To enforce the income tax sections of the Finance Acts and maximise revenue.'

'That's part of it.'

Ade frowned.

'I'm sorry?'

'Don't be.' The woman behind the desk, she hadn't introduced herself, smiled, her lips compressed. 'You are a

29

servant of Her Majesty. Your job is primarily to implement government policy. Government policy is decided by my Minister. Check your job description.'

Denny nodded again.

Ade said, 'Yes.'

'Good. So long as you understand.'

The woman tapped a file on the desk.

'The Webster Consultancy. Much respected. In some ways a City bellwether. I understand your enquiries have been aggressive. My Minister wishes us to be seen as a business-friendly government. We wish to have a more cooperative relationship between tax-payers and the Revenue. There's too much suspicion, too much regulation. We plan to move towards a revenue framework guided by an industry code of practice.'

Ade said nothing. She thought of the envelope: *whose pay-roll are you on?* There was a silence. Denny spoke for the first time.

'All my staff understand their duties.'

Colin understood it all right, thought Ade, he found out which side his bread was buttered on pretty soon. Morwen understood it differently.

'So long as that is understood.' The woman smiled but her eyes were like gun-metal.

Assent? Is that all you want? You want us to give up so you can outsource the Revenue to your accountancy friends.

Ade relaxed her grip on the sides of her chair. The woman stared at her as if weighing her up.

'There's another thing.'

Ade thought of Webster, of the money in the envelope slipped down the bottom of her brief-case, of the expression on his face. She wasn't going to mention the money.

'You've been associating with,' she flipped open the file, 'a Mr Paul Affarn.'

'That's nothing to do with the Revenue, it's my private life. He's not a close friend anyway.'

The woman snapped the file shut and kept her hand on it.

'Of course. Nothing to do with the Revenue.'

She glanced at Denny.

'I think we're done.'

She picked up the file and walked to the door, ignoring Denny's outstretched hand, then paused and swung round.

'You're coming up for review aren't you, Ms Corey? For a grade six?'

'Yes.'

The grey eyes were fixed on her. Ade felt something important was being said.

'That's often the most difficult promotion. Especially for a woman.'

She pulled the door open.

'Good day. Don't escort me.'

The door clicked shut. Denny stood for a minute looking at Ade. She snapped on the light.

'Special advisors,' she said, 'I hate them. A cooperative relationship with business.' She sniffed. 'There's our side and there's their side and that's all there is.'

'Is there a problem?'

Denny motioned her to the chair. 'Your work is excellent. You have increased revenue from the consultancy sector year on year. It's the most difficult sector.'

'It was really Morwen's model.'

Denny closed her eyes and Ade saw how tired she was. She ran her hand across her face. 'Morwen Archer. I couldn't do anything, not with all of them closing ranks. You understand that, don't you?'

'No one blames you.'

Denny looked down. The window behind her was fully in shadow. Ade couldn't make out the bricks on the wall opposite. She wished she could put out a hand and touch Denny's shoulder. Not appropriate.

'Truly,' she said. 'No one blames you.'

Denny grunted. 'Give yourself some credit. You worked on that model and it was the best thing anyone's ever done in this office. Not a good idea to say so at the time. It's not on your record, at least I made sure of that.'

She paused and continued: 'Webster's a rattlesnake. But I can't pass this request for a special audit.'

'We could ask,' said Ade. She kept her voice level. 'The evidence is there. You should see the artwork in his office: a quarter of a million upwards each picture.'

'Yes. They love to flaunt it and when you ask where they got it, someone gave it them, it was a win on the spread-betting, they got it at a boot fair. But that's not the point. I'm doing this for you. When Morwen tried it, you saw what happened. They faked those charges, I'm sure of it, but there was no way I could stop them.'

'This is different; everything adds up, there's a hole in those accounts you could drive a bus through.'

Denny sat there staring at the stack of files on her desk.

'You don't understand what we're up against. Not really. They hate paying tax. They'll do absolutely anything to avoid it. It's not just money, it's power; it's who they are. They have to win, always. We can only make progress slowly.'

'I understand.' Ade paused. 'I was the last one of us to see her. In Bronzefield. I'm sorry,' she added quickly as she saw the hurt on Denny's face. 'I didn't mean it like that.' She found she had her hand on the desk just next to Denny's. She slid it back.

'It's OK, Ade. You did everything you could. And more. That's why there won't be a special audit. We're not going to make trouble.' Denny sighed. 'Then there's the reassignment. Grounds of incompatibility. But it's your field.'

'Personal incompatibility, not technical incompatibility.'

'Yes. He's a slimy rattlesnake. But we're professionals.' Denny stared through the window into the blackness. 'That special advisor. She's right you know. Grade six is the hardest one. Then you're on the inside, Head Office material. I never made it and look at me now.'

'People respect you,' said Ade.

'You have to go to the meeting with the accountant. Just do everything by the book. No fancy models. Business-friendly. You'll fight another day. When you're a grade six you'll have more influence. Things will get better.'

It seemed to Ade that the shadows deepened outside the window. She didn't say anything. Denny touched the back of her hand. 'Everything's OK, is it?'

Ade straightened her back. 'Of course. Shouldn't it be?'

'None of my business, it's just…you were a good friend of Morwen's weren't you?'

'Yes. I tried to be.'

Denny was standing very close to her. 'I trust you, Ade. I'll try to help. But some things are outside my control. These people are very powerful. Take care.'

She held open the door. Ade saw how everyone in the office glanced up from their screens and looked down again. She ignored all of them. She'd said nothing about the money. Business-friendly.

7

Ade sat on a comfortable upright chair, the lap-top open on her knees like a barrier, watching Webster as his eyes followed the blonde young woman in the tight cream dress with the coffee tray. The sun streamed through the picture window, the river sparkled and the buildings opposite rose up like a white marble cliff. The secretary set down the tray and turned to Ade, a professional smile on her face.

'No thanks,' said Ade, smiling at her, 'I'm fine.'

The secretary bobbed her head and poured coffee for Webster and Ms Devi, the accountant. Webster touched her arm.

'A little cream.'

He kept his hand on her arm and, as she leant forward, he slid it towards her breast. She jerked back, and a white tongue licked out from the jug and slopped onto the carpet.

'Careful, Jessica.' He pulled the handkerchief out of his top pocket. 'Here, mop it up.'

He looked round at Ms Devi who was busy with something in her briefcase and, quite deliberately, at Ade. She stared back. *Stones, think of his eyes as stones.* After a long pause he looked up at the secretary. The young woman took the handkerchief, bunched it in her hand, bent and dabbed once at the floor.

'Not like that, get down to it.'

He put his hand on her shoulder, pushing her down to her knees. Ms Devi was still rummaging in her brief-case. Ade stared at him, horrified.

'That's right,' said Webster. He sounded almost happy. Ade was on her feet. 'Mr Webster, do not harass your staff.'

Webster smiled at her. 'I forget, you civil servants with your codes and your rules-books and your fuss. We're all a team here, we have our little jokes. It's all right Jessica, you can go.'

Ade felt her throat constricted. The young woman glanced at Ade, blushed, and moved towards the door. Webster continued: 'Sorry about all that.'

Jessica ducked her head and closed the door softly.

'Women,' said Webster and rolled his eyes to the accountant. She ignored him, found what she was looking for in her briefcase and snapped it shut.

Ade took a deep breath. Business-friendly: 'Thank you for inviting me to your office. Now perhaps we should consider the accounts.'

'Of course,' said Webster, 'Glad you could come. I hope I can think of you as part of the team, too.'

He gestured, 'It's all technical stuff, Sita here deals with that, she's good with numbers. I'm just the salesman.'

Ms Devi smiled quickly at Ade and looked down again at the spreadsheets. She was slightly built with eyes that reminded Ade of olives and skin the colour of dark syrup. She wore a neat trouser suit and used a biro to point at the sheet in front of her.

'Please observe.' She spoke precisely, with the accent of a leading university, 'transactions, costs, fully itemised, depreciation, carry over from our loss last year and there is the net figure.'

She tapped the biro on the sheet again and glanced up at Webster.

'All duly certified.'

Ade felt their eyes on her. There must be something wrong. The cash flows into the Webster Consultancy exceeded those shown in the accounts by many times. Start low key. 'My analysis indicates that the sums handled by your firm are larger than those shown here.'

'That's a mistake,' said Webster, rather sharply. 'We're only a small concern; just one office, a handful of staff. Old-established. You mustn't confuse us with our overseas subsidiary.' He smiled. 'That's based in another jurisdiction.'

Ade met his eyes and held them. 'I need to see the details.'

'It's a nested spread-sheet.' Ms Devi clicked on a tab, filling the screen with tiny numbers. 'It's all certified of course. If you look at the bottom line,' she scrolled down a thousand lines and increased the font size, 'you can see: money in, money out. The transactions are elsewhere.'

Webster gestured towards the screen: 'We pay all the tax required by the law in the jurisdiction where the transactions take place. No double taxation – that's the rule isn't it? Wouldn't be fair.'

He had stopped smiling at her. He almost looked bored.

'Yes,' said Ade. 'The Caymans I believe.' *Perhaps named after the caiman, a close relative of the alligator.*

'Why not? A well-developed financial services sector

there. Excellent location for global business contacts. Low office costs.'

This is all pointless, Ade thought. So long as the Treasury allows Webster to off-shore his profits to tax havens, all my work, Morwen's work, is for nothing. She felt a sense of disgust, as if she were being forced to touch something dirty.

She continued with her prepared script. 'There's the loss carried forward from last year,' she said. 'That more or less wipes out your net profit.'

Ms Devi glanced at her, then down at the sheet. 'Yes,' she said, and coughed. Webster cut in.

'It's a risk business, up and down. I made big losses last year on the overseas business and I set them off this year.'

He patted the accountant on the back and let his hand linger there. 'That's the rule, isn't it?'

Ade looked away out over the river, over the city the towers gleaming in winter sunshine, the greatest financial centre in Europe. 'Yes,' she said. 'That's the rule.'

Webster rubbed his hands together. 'Good, that's that. We can tidy up the details by email.'

He rose.

'Now let's eat.' His gesture included both of them. 'You'll come won't you, Adeline?'

She felt his hand on her arm.

'Yes. Thank you.'

That's in the rules now, too, she thought. *Saying 'Thank You' to them. Business-friendly*. Ms Devi picked up her briefcase. Webster stood back for Ade to precede him through the door.

'No,' she said. 'After you.'

She noticed the fair-haired young woman who'd brought the coffee standing behind an oak desk to one side of the reception area, the appointments book open in front of her, her eyes fixed on the page.

'Just a moment. I'll catch you up.'

She walked across to the desk. 'I don't think we were properly introduced.' She held out her hand. 'I'm Adeline Corey.'

The young woman flushed. She was strikingly beautiful with a heart-shaped face, dark blue eyes and rich blond hair that looked as if it had been polished. 'I'm Jessica Dean. You know, you're the first visitor to this office who's introduced herself properly to me.'

She put down her pen and shook hands. Her fingers were cold, slender with perfect nails.

'I just wanted to talk to you. You know you don't have to put up with it. There are organisations that will help you. He's harassing you.'

Jessica looked up at Ade with full eyes. She spoke more confidently that Ade expected. 'Thank you. You've got it all wrong, you know. People like Webster expect to behave in a certain way. I can handle him. And the money's good.'

'If you ever need any help, you know where to find me.'

Jessica smiled and glanced round. The desk was clear apart from the register. 'Thank you, and I mean it. Most of them treat me like I'm part of the furniture. Here. Christmas present.'

She offered the biro she'd been writing with.

'Thanks,' said Ade. 'Thank you very much.'

She took it, an expensive ball-point pen. Silvery metal, with a hint of gold in the clip and RW engraved in italics.

'One for the collection.'

She slipped it into her pocket.

'Have another, they're good pens,' said Jessica. 'Nothing else to give you just now.'

'Thanks.'

Webster stood by the lift.

'Come on,' he said. He was standing too close to her. She edged away from him. She felt the anger starting to glow inside her, embers among the tinder.

'Like I said, Adeline, you mustn't take things to heart. It's a game. Jessica does what she's paid for. She's good at some things.' He patted her arm. 'Just like everyone else. Everyone on the team.'

'Does that include the Minister's special advisor?'

'Which one?' he grinned at her. 'Come on Adeline, money's money.'

'I would prefer it if you would address me as Ms Corey. Let us be clear. I'm only here on instructions. The Revenue wishes to show a human face to its cases.'

'Of course, and you're doing your job very well. Nothing to stop us enjoying ourselves, though. Besides, money's money.'

8

They were at a restaurant two streets away, next to a small hotel, no sign outside, just a liveried porter on the steps who saluted them. Webster stood back to allow the two women through the door. Ms Devi went first and Ade followed behind. She felt his breath on her neck. *Why am I here?* she thought. *Same answer as last time – you don't enjoy it but you get paid for it. Just like a …professional, Denny called it. He thinks he's bought me, but he hasn't.*

A plump man in evening dress came towards them, a sheaf of menus in his hand, smiling past her. 'Mr Webster,' he said. 'Always a pleasure. Welcome!'

'Table for three, George. Somewhere quiet.'

He took Ade by the elbow, steering her after the waiter. She had an impression of space, of warm humid air, of arches, of gold wall lights and mouldings, of tables scattered across what must once have been a ball-room, a splendid chandelier above each one. All round them rose the noise of conversation. Nobody saw anything unusual, a couple and a friend going out for a meal, obviously straight from the office. They were led to a table set back in an alcove.

'George is one of my clients, you know,' said Webster when they were seated. 'Owes me a favour. Now what do you say to some bubbly?'

He took out his handkerchief, the scent of expensive perfume wafting towards her.

'Mr Webster, this isn't what I imagined. I can't accept something like this, it's far too expensive.'

He leaned back in his chair, smiling.

'Nonsense! Just a meal at a quiet restaurant. You work hard, you deserve it. Sita's happy here, aren't you?'

Ms Devi nodded without smiling and looked down at the menu. Webster ignored her, snapped his fingers for George and rattled off a list of dishes. Ade had never eaten so well. She'd never eaten truffles before, nor sturgeon, nor cavy, nor Patagonian strawberries. She'd only had the kind of champagne you get in supermarkets, and not much of that.

A glow of warmth spread through her, softening everything. She caught herself thinking of Paul and his quick nervous eyes, and smiled. And there was the man opposite her with his expansive gestures and complacent mouth, the man she had to watch like she was a snake. No, he was the snake – she had to make sure she kept her head. Somewhere her pulse was beating loudly. She kept her eyes fixed on him and talked about the Revenue and the City. The wine was so smooth you could drink it like lemonade.

Ms Devi's phone buzzed. She glanced at it then answered the call, turning away from the table and speaking rapidly in a language Ade didn't recognise. 'I'm terribly sorry, Mr Webster. I really have to go. My son...'

'That's a pity,' he said, 'just when we were getting another bottle.'

She turned to Ade, and held out her hand. 'A pleasure

Ms Corey. I'm sorry to appear rude. I hope we can look forward to a speedy resolution of the accounts.'

It was the most she'd said all evening.

She looked directly at Webster for the first time. Ade caught him nod to her and she was striding out of the restaurant before Ade could wish her good evening. Webster smiled across the table at her. She stood up.

'Don't go,' he said. 'Aren't you forgetting something? There was that business with the Christmas card.'

She frowned. 'What Christmas card, Mr Webster?'

She met his eyes.

'Don't be silly. There aren't so many fifty-pound notes that you can't trace them quite quickly. Particularly when they crop up in unusual places. Like a gang of homeless people, drunk as lords, using them to buy litre bottles of whisky. I've paid. Haven't I? Fair's fair.'

His eyes were fixed on hers. *Poor Johnno*, she thought. Webster felt in his hip pocket and slipped out a snug pigskin wallet. His eyes still on hers, he extracted a fifty-pound note, laid it on the table, tore it in half lengthways, and held up the pieces at shoulder height. She straightened her back, the blood racing though her veins. Revenge is a dish best served cold. Whoever said that didn't know hatred.

'Of course, fifty pounds means nothing to me,' he said softly.

The waiter was standing next to him.

'Got any sellotape, George? Here's another. And another. And another. On account.'

When George had gone he added: 'George is a very good witness in court. He sees things you wouldn't believe.

So just enjoy your meal. Business-friendly, as your boss at the Revenue says.' He grinned and left the wallet on the table. 'Ah, here's the wine. He took the bottle out of the ice-bucket. 'Drink up.'

Her thoughts were coming more slowly and everything was pleasantly blurred. The relaxed, comfortable feeling suffused her whole body. She was in a café with Paul, somewhere off Tooley Street and they kept bringing sausages and plates of chips, wonderful chips, crisp and delicate, and bottles of champagne. Music was playing and he was on his feet. He was inviting her to dance, she was a wonderful dancer.

Then a door slammed behind her, cutting off the noise of the restaurant, and Paul's face was pressed against the glass panels, like Morwen against the glass screen in Bronzefield, and the air was suddenly cold and Webster had his arm wrapped round her, he was guiding her into a lift.

'Where are we going?' she said.

He pulled her against him. She felt dizzy.

'Come along, there's a good girl,' he grunted.

The doors whispered shut and he pushed her back against the mirrored wall of the lift. Anger surged through her. She felt the harsh bristles on his face scratching at her skin, the weight of him pressing her backwards, she smelt the odour of wine and sweat and tobacco hanging round him. She twisted her head and the roll of fat at his neck pressed against her lips, stifling her. She felt she couldn't breathe; panic flared within her.

She bit at him as hard as she could, and tasted the blood, salt in her mouth.

'Get off me!' she shouted. She shoved at his chest with both hands.

'Now don't be like that,' he said, slurring the words slightly. 'Think yourself lucky. That's good money you've had.'

She could see blood on his neck smudging his collar.

The lift stopped and the doors crashed open. He pushed her forward, onto the landing, his hands groping at her body. She twisted round towards him. His face lurched towards her and she punched at his mouth. He seized her wrist and forced her hand down onto his body, exhaling a stale smell of half-digested food in her face. Nausea overwhelmed her. She jack-knifed forward and vomited, coughing, the acid burning in her throat.

She felt him stagger backwards, snorting, and she stumbled sideways into the lift. Her fingers were on the buttons. He grabbed at the closing door, pulling at it to force it open. She spat thick phlegm onto his hand. It made no difference. She steadied herself against the corner of the lift and slipped off a shoe. She stared as the woman in the mirror opposite her swung up her hand and smashed the heel down onto the fingers. He screamed and the hand disappeared leaving a smear of blood on the brass-work.

9

Ade leaned against the wall of the alley, watching him as he moved away from her. He reeled into the gutter, then back onto the pavement. He'd tied a silk scarf round his throat for a bandage and he had his right hand in his overcoat pocket. Her heart pounded in her chest and her fingers curled as if she had them wrapped round his throat. She tasted the blood in her mouth, iron and bone, and spat. The road was wet after rain, the streetlights glared down on them, glistening yellow on the tarmac. There was no-one about and she was certain that he had no idea she was following him. She'd waited in the shadows, watching the hotel entrance, not moving, not thinking, just standing there, she didn't know for how long, until he came out. Revenge is a dish best eaten cold.

After a while she pushed herself upright and moved forward. She had no idea what she was going to do. She stared at him, the scarf almost cutting into his neck, the exposed band of soft skin, the broad back, the rounded shoulders, the expensive shoes stumbling through the puddles. She hated him.

He turned a corner onto a wider road and she ran a few paces so as not to lose him. She shrank back from the brightness of the street, the light spilling from the windows of the pub opposite. A group of people were striding towards her, she could hear them chattering, the fair-haired girl on the end walking sideways so the others could see her, waving an arm. She could see no sign of Webster.

The girl pulled at one of the men and the group veered across the road towards the pub not looking where they were going. A cyclist in pink lycra swerved, skidded, recovered and sped away.

He's in there with those drunken louts, thought Ade. *They're like him, all of them. I can't do a thing.*

That's what she hated most. There was no way you could get back at them, they always made the rules, they owned it all and you were on the outside, you counted for nothing.

She heard a splashing, hissing noise to her right and edged forward. There was another alley to the side of a shop. She saw a dented metal bin with cardboard boxes piled against it. He was the other side of it, holding onto a drain-pipe, his back to her, pissing. He retched and spat.

She stared at him and moved forward into the mouth of the alley. He was no more than five feet away from her. He grunted and hunched forward, the stream of urine spattering onto the stones, the sharp animal smell gusting back at her. The band of white skin at his neck gleamed in the light from the street behind her. The image of a knife, with a riveted wooden handle and a long slender blade, sharp, serrated on one side, like the knife in her kitchen drawer, only gripped tightly in her fist, filled her mind. She thought of the knife in her hand, her fist pounding, pounding against his back. She flexed her fingers and moved forward, feeling in her pocket, making no noise at all. On the street behind her someone was shouting for a taxi.

He grunted something, she couldn't make out the words, then she caught them: 'Bitch. Paid good money. She owes me.'

He spat again. The metal pen was in her fist, sleek, gleaming in the yellow streetlight. She rammed the point hard against his neck.

The pissing stopped. There was a second of absolute silence, then he said, hardly above a whisper, 'Don't hurt me.'

She increased the pressure on the pen very slightly. She stared at the pit it made in the fat skin, stretched tight. She thought of dimples, of a baby's plumpness. She thought of how much more force it would need to break through, to jab into his neck, for blood to spurt up hot onto her hand, to trickle round under the scarf, to join up with the blood from where she'd bitten him. She thought of Morwen's face that morning when she'd finished the Model, the brightness in her eyes.

'I've got money,' said Webster. 'Take it, all of it.'

The soft flesh of his neck, drawn taut round the tip of the pen, filled her gaze. This was the feeling of power they had, when they casually asked you for a drink, when they took you out, when they ran their hand across you, when they pinched and poked you, when they treated you like flesh on a market-stall, something they'd paid for.

'I don't want your money,' she growled in a deep unfamiliar voice. She twisted the pen slightly and increased the pressure.

48

He was fumbling at his wrist.

'Take my watch. Franck Muller – best watch in the world.'

It dangled from his fingers, light from the street behind them glinting on the dial. She knocked it to the ground with her free hand.

'I don't want your watch.'

She twisted the pen ever so slightly. He gave a strange whimpering groan.

'Get the coat off,' she said, 'the jacket.'

He shrugged them off. She grabbed them with her free hand and let them fall behind her.

'Now. Drop your trousers.'

There was a burst of noise as the pub door opened.

'Don't turn round!'

They both stood there, not moving, listening to the voices fading away down the street. She twisted the pen another half turn. He jerked sideways against the wall, sobbing.

'Quiet! 'She pressed slightly harder. She could see how tight the skin was about the tip, creases running down towards the nib from all sides.

He had his trousers round his ankles. Clumsily, he lifted one foot and shook it free, then the other. 'What do you want?' he said. 'I'll get money, more money.'

'I don't want your money.' She kept her voice deep.

'Money's everything. You got money, they come running. Bitches. You can do anything you like with them, anything at all.'

She jabbed at him with all her strength and felt the resistance give and the metal cylinder slide into his neck, like a skewer sliding into meat. He jerked forward, ripping it out of her hand, doubling up. The pen stuck out of his neck like the hilt of a knife. She slapped her hands against him, feeling them smack against the soft flesh, braced herself and shoved at him as hard as she could. He fell forward onto the cobblestones and lay there groaning, twisting his head from side to side, the pale flesh of his thighs splayed wide.

She reached down and snatched up the clothes. Then she took a pace forward and laid her fingers on the pen. She could feel a faint vibration, rhythmic, the beat of his pulse. She was hardly breathing at all. She gripped tighter and pulled. It slid smoothly out. A dark pool of blood welled up, spilled over and ran down onto the cobblestones. She backed away against the cardboard boxes, grabbed at the stack and pulled them down on him, turned and ran.

10

She was on Waterloo Bridge, leaning over the parapet out near the middle. It was late and they'd turned off the streetlights. The water surged under her, loud in the darkness. Once a taxi cruised past, slowed for her and accelerated away. She could smell the river, dank, cold, salt as blood.

She had no idea of the time. The sky above her was filled with clouds, the moon somewhere faraway up above them. She'd been running, through streets and alleys, onwards, between streetlights, trying to keep away from the people, all those faces staring at her. She dodged round a man in a business suit who waved a wine bottle as he grabbed at her with a black-gloved hand. She ran, zig-zagging through crowds, onto a brightly-lit street, into traffic that jerked to a halt, a driver getting out of his car to shout something. Once she crossed a park, grass under her feet and a gravel path, a long dark building on the skyline. She'd run along by the river in darkness with the gush of the water beside her for what seemed miles. She stood on the bridge, gasping, her feet aching, the breath sobbing in her throat. She stared upstream, over the dark water, past the bulk of the Houses of Parliament, away into the sky, beyond all this. She felt sick.

They'd find him, they'd check his diary, Sita Devi would talk to them or George and they'd be after her. She had to think straight. *How did you go on the run? Where was her passport, did you need a passport? Were there still countries she could hide, where they wouldn't find her? Would people think she was a refugee?*

She'd lost most of the clothing, but she still had the jacket and the pen. She looked down at it, snug in her hand. No blood on it at all. Hard to think how powerful it had made her. She should drop it now, watch it cut into the dark water with no sound, like a dart. She clicked the point out and back and slipped it into her pocket. It hardly showed.

The jacket was well-made, nearly new. Armani. She lifted it and felt the weight of the wallet in the pocket. She drew out the wallet and let the jacket slide over the parapet. It fell, opening into a ghostly shape before disappearing into the water.

She opened the wallet. It was stuffed with fifty-pound notes, a thick wad. Maybe Webster didn't like to keep it in the bank; too many records. Maybe this was just small change. Her fingers touched something caught up with it, small and thin and hard: the wristwatch he'd said was Franck Muller.

She held the watch in her hand and felt it ticking against her palm, like a pulse. The second hand, thin as a hair, swept on. She rolled the watch over and made out *'RW for services rendered – you bastard!'* engraved on the back of the case in elaborate italics. She held it there for a while. £10,000? £20,000? Then she flipped it back, raised her hand and smashed the watch face down onto

52

the concrete parapet of the bridge. Fragments of glass and metal shimmered silently down, into the water below. A footstep sounded on the bridge somewhere behind her, in the darkness. She slipped the money and the shattered watch into her jacket pocket beside the pen and hurled the wallet as far as she could into the darkness.

She started walking south as fast as she could, trying to keep where the shadows were darkest. She heard the noise again and looked back, but she couldn't see anyone. She half-ran for a few paces then fell into a walk. She felt the breath coming in her throat.

She was on the embankment, the bulk of the National Theatre rearing up behind her, a waterfall of Christmas lights cascading down it. She felt exhausted, she wanted to be somewhere dark where she could hide. She moved towards the shadows under the bridge, stopping to catch her breath. There was someone standing there, Paul. He stepped forward.

'Are you all right?'

'I'll be OK.'

She halted and stood there looking at him.

'Don't follow me.'

He looked down. 'I want to. I seen you running. You don't half go.'

'It's not a joke.' She was so tired she could hardly stand up. She leant against the stone. 'Just forget you saw me.'

She heard footsteps walking firmly towards them. 'Come on,' said Paul. 'Quiet.'

He grabbed her wrist and pulled her into the shadows under the bridge. The stonework was cold and rough against her hand. She felt he was on her side. He led her round a corner and up a stone stairway. The boots came to a halt.

They could hear voices. Paul crouched, drawing her down beside him, and they peered over the parapet. She saw two policemen, bulky in their stab vests, down below them. The policemen looked round and one of them flashed a torch under the bridge. Then they moved off, in step, towards the National Theatre.

'City of London,' said Paul, 'Like the ones in the café that night, City of London. You can tell by the red and white arm-bands. What are they doing here? Their area's north of the river. Like I said, you need someone to look out for you.'

She lay back against the bridge. The cold of the pavement seeped into her. Her whole body ached, she felt she could hardly move. She still had Paul's hand clasped tightly in hers.

'Paul,' she said. 'I think I just killed someone.'

He put his arm round her. 'You ain't a killer. You just ain't.

'I stabbed him in the neck. With a metal biro. I could feel his pulse through it.' She found she was crying. She didn't want to cry, she wiped at her eyes. He felt in his pocket and pulled something out.

'Here.' He squatted in front of her and stroked the tissue across her face, across her eye-lids very carefully, very gently. She felt his thin fingers caressing her across her cheeks. For a moment the delicacy of his finger-tips was all she could think of. 'We gotta be careful. Who was he? Does anyone know?'

She held onto his arm. 'You don't know him. His

name's Webster, he's some bastard in the city. He tried to rape me.'

Paul whistled. After a moment he said: 'Webster. You're some girl. We got to think this through.'

'Best thing is you forget you met me. I'll be OK.' She reached out for the parapet but didn't have the strength to pull herself to her feet.

'I said I was looking out for you. I want to.'

'I've made enough trouble already.'

'You're all in, girl. You need somewhere to rest. You better lean on me.'

He slipped his arm round her waist, stood up and helped her to her feet. She felt she'd done something irrevocable, something wrong, and she'd feel the guilt for the rest of her life, but now someone understood and would forgive her. She slung her right arm round his shoulders and they moved slowly forward.

11

Huge clouds filled the sky and the moon was a sallow glow behind them. Paul had his arm round her waist, supporting her. They'd been walking for a long time. They'd gone east, mainly along alleyways between the buildings, and away from the Thames. Now they were in an area of run-down four storey terraces. They'd been built for the gentry when this was a fashionable neighbourhood, stone steps to the front door, portico, attics for the servants and a mews at the back for the carriage.

Paul halted and glanced down the street. 'Nearly there.' He half-pulled half-led her into a passageway, dark between terrace blocks. She could see they were empty. The windows were boarded up and there were graffiti along the wall, with pound signs trampling on people. The building they were next to had once been a shop. She could make out the sign: Minsky's Gentlemen's Outfitters, in faded gold paint above the shuttered window.

'It's Webster's,' he said. 'The whole block. Finger in every pie.' He put a hand to his forehead. 'Thank you, Mr Webster – bastard. You're not the only one hates him'

He leaned against a wooden gate which gave and swung open. They slipped through it into an overgrown garden, with walls on all sides. He pushed the gate back and jammed a plank of wood against it.

Ade leaned on the wall and looked up at the house. She could make out a dim light, flickering like a candle in one of the windows. Paul whistled twice. She heard a noise and the back door was pushed open.

'Come on,' said a voice and a large man with a beard stood on the threshold. She recognised Johnno. He stood staring at her.

'It's all right, Johnno,' said Paul, gripping his arm. 'She's on our side.'

'I know that. It's just… you told us this place was safe. No-one knew.'

'It's all right. Let's get inside.'

Paul took her hand and led her through the door.

The room was lit by two candles on the wooden table in front of her. It seemed to be crammed full of people, all of them staring at her. There was the close smell of too many people in one place. She could hear whispering; they were talking about her but she was so tired she couldn't take it all in. She was warm, sitting at a table, leaning against Paul. She'd have to tell him everything: about Webster, about the alleyway, the fold of flesh at his neck, the way the pen felt when she gripped it in her hand. She'd do that soon. Outside, the moon showed through a crack in the clouds and she could see more of the garden through the window. There was a greenhouse against the back wall. One of the panes was shattered but she could see that the wood was newly-painted. Some leeks poked up in a tilled plot next to it where the overgrowth had been cut back.

She looked from face to face, trying to remember names. There was Eileen, painfully thin with deep lines each side of her mouth and intense dark eyes, her fingers always restless, always picking; Mariska, slender, with paint on her jeans, who waved and smiled at her; and Ilah, dark, effusive and deep-voiced. Ade later found out he could sing in a way that lifted your soul out of your body. Flat Alan looked up, grunted and gave her one brilliant smile, then hid again in the hood of his jacket. Ethan, ex-army, muttered 'Hi' and went on working on something in the corner. And there was Johnno, of course, who had remembered the fifty pounds and was still saying thanks.

'Come on Johnno, cup of tea, let's have a cup of tea,' said Paul. 'And bread if there is any?'

'Yeah, I been baking,' said Ilah. 'Paul always loves my bread,' he told Ade, 'Nothing better.'

He placed a loaf and a knife in front of them and, as an afterthought, a small block of butter on a dish. Paul drew the knife across the loaf and the smell of fresh bread welled up, embracing all of them.

'Hey,' said Paul. 'We gonna eat!'

That's a slice each, thought Ade. *If you're lucky.*

Johnno slapped down the mugs of tea.

'This is so good,' said Ade, drawing in a full breath. She couldn't help smiling. Mariska and Ilah smiled back at her. The others were busy with the food. She began to feel more alive. They would look after her. They didn't know what she'd done. Paul would help her, they wouldn't find out. Maybe they wouldn't care. She'd find somewhere to hide.

'There's more,' said Paul. 'There's always more, more for my friends in our house.'

He waved an arm embracing all of them and Ade saw him, king in his castle. She wasn't going to tell him that the milk was sour. She drank the tea anyway.

'I used to run the homeless project,' said Paul to her. 'That's where I met everyone. Then they took the grant away. So we were all out on the street. Then we found this place.'

'Yeah,' said Johnno. 'Took it away.'

He thrust his head close to them.

'S'all right, Johnno.' Paul slipped his arm round Johnno's shoulders and pulled his head down. 'We're here now.'

He turned to Ade.

'It's not like most people think, you know. We all work. Eileen washes up at that café, Ilah's on the embankment all day everyday outside the Festival Hall doing the statues, Alan helps out in the soup kitchen, Mariska's an artist. There are waiters here, and a shop assistant, and casual workers, labourers, all the people London needs. Johnno can carry a hod on a good day, can't you Johnno?'

Johnno grinned and gave a thumbs-up sign.

Paul opened his hands.

'Just none of us can afford the rent with the likes of Webster around. Or the deposit.'

'You're right there,' a small brindled man with sharp eyes and a pointed face said. He had been sitting in the shadow at the foot of the stairs the whole time, watching. 'That's why we gotta be careful.'

Ade couldn't see much of the man's face, just the bright points of his eyes fixed on her. Then he leaned forward and she saw black hair and pockmarks all down one cheek.

'You've got money. What you want to come here for?'
He spoke with a Belfast accent.

'Don't worry, Casey, Ade's all right.' Paul said. 'She's
with me.'

'Yeah she's with Paul,' said Johnno and a murmur ran
round.

'But we don't want no-one else. We're OK here.'

Casey was on his feet glaring round like he'd take on
all of them. A shadow ran across the room. Ade realised
someone had walked past the window. There was a double
knock and the door banged open and a wave of relief ran
through everyone. Casey sat down again.

A tall, brown-skinned woman, with calm dark eyes
entered. She had an oval face and was dressed in a blue
fleece jacket a size too large for her.

'Hi everyone,' she said, 'I got bacon.'

'Nadia,' said Paul. 'She always wanted to be a nurse in
her country. Then there was the war and she was lucky.
She got out. Now she works in the kitchen in St George's.
So we get anything left over.'

Nadia smiled round the room, waved to Paul, then
saw Ade. She came forward and held out her hand.

Ade took it.

'I'm pleased to meet you,' said Nadia. The dark eyes
stayed on Ade. Ade felt her hand warm and safe in Nadia's.

'Had a hard time, haven't you?' said Nadia. 'You sit
easy; this is a good man. I'll get bacon sandwiches.'

'There ain't no bread,' said Ethan. 'We ate it.'

'There's bacon.'

Ethan stirred in his corner. 'We gotta talk. You brought
someone back, Paul. You shouldn't have done that. We

60

always said: first rule, never let anyone know where this place is.'

'Yeah,' said Casey. 'And she got money. Johnno's seen it. What's she doing here?'

Nadia clattered the pan on the stove. The fragrant smell of frying bacon filled the room. Ade found it almost overwhelming.

Mariska raised her voice: 'This is different. Can't you see? She needs help. Paul wouldn't bring her if she didn't need help, would you?'

'That's the truth.' He looked round the room. 'I just want to help her.'

'She ain't got the cops after her, has she?' asked Casey. 'She'll bring trouble.'

'What you say, sister?' said Nadia. 'You look like you had trouble.'

'I... Please let me stay. I want to stay. I've nowhere else to go.'

'Lots of people got nowhere to go,' said Ilah.

'Not the worst thing.' Everyone looked round. Alan was speaking in a deep preacher's voice. Ade guessed he didn't talk a lot. 'Worst thing... how people treat you when you got nowhere and you ask them to help you. How they look at you.'

There was a murmur of agreement round the room. Paul stood up and glared at them all. He looked so small, standing there with the candle-light glowing on his face and the darkness behind him, thought Ade, like a painting she'd once seen in the National.

'Someone treated her very bad. She can stay one night. OK? Just one night.'

Nadia lifted the pan and tipped the bacon onto a plate. 'Yeah. Now let's eat.'

Casey wolfed down a long rasher of bacon. Ade felt his eyes on her. She shivered. She was safe, for tonight. She didn't take any of the bacon.

Ade felt she was at peace. She hadn't felt like this for a long time. She lay back on a mattress against the wall in the corner of an empty room up a flight of wooden stairs. Light filtered in through an uncurtained window.

Nadia tucked the quilt gently round her cheeks. 'Close your eyes. Sleep.'

Ade felt herself sinking down into the bed, into darkness. Somewhere she could hear singing. A memory welled up from far away, darkness, a warm bed and someone singing.

She opened her eyes. Nadia was sitting there in the moonlight, singing gently to her, singing her to sleep. The words she didn't recognise, sounds from a language spoken far away, but there was comfort in them, and understanding.

'Nadia,' she said. 'I've done something, something dreadful.'

Nadia placed a hand on her wrist.

'Sleep now. We'll talk about it tomorrow.'

12

Ade lay there, warm in her bed, staring at the window. The clouds had gone. Nadia was next to her, fast asleep. Paul lay curled up on a mattress on the far side of the room, snoring gently. There was no movement anywhere in the house. She was the only one left awake. She felt as if she was on guard.

She stared as a silver moon rose up, floating up over the streets and towers of London, shining down on parks and gardens, on the river twisting below it, a glittering snake, the serpent that tied all London together.

She raised herself on one elbow and looked across at Paul. He seemed so young, his skin smooth as chocolate, the hair lying back from his face. A tiny whorl of baby-hair twisted round just behind his ear. He stirred and murmured something. Should she wake him? There was something she had to explain to him. About how she'd wanted to kill Webster. Then she'd have to go. Not now. She'd let him sleep on. She lay there watching over him.

Ade thought of how she'd lived in this city all her life, of the suburbs long ago, of her mother and how she would make up stories. She remembered a birthday with cake and a real theatre, the stage splendid and dazzling, with a boy who could fly, played by a girl, who saved them all and smiled down at everybody and once just at her. Everything had been so much more vivid, so much more real than the streets outside and she had cried when she had to go home.

She thought of the school and the college and of her life with friends from so many different places; and of that interview, when Caroline, the sixth-form teacher, had explained how it all changed now and how it got serious and the choices you made might transform your whole life. She remembered how pressured things had been and how pointless, the routine spreadsheet work in the office all day, the bright point of Birkbeck in the evenings. Then she was a graduate, BA (Accounting) and there was the thick white envelope with her name on it. Everyone had been so pleased that the civil service had accepted her, her parents, her sister, Caroline, her tutor, and, most of all, her friends. She thought of that day when she'd put on her new clothes and travelled on the familiar unfamiliar underground train and arrived at the office on a bright wind-swept street half an hour before anyone else. That was when she first met Morwen.

Morwen. She remembered how she felt standing there alone in the lobby. She took one deep breath, expelled it, and, before she could think, swung open the double doors. The office was right in front of her, the rows of desks, and the figure coming towards her with her hand outstretched. Later the other new staff had all told her how lucky she was to have Morwen as her mentor.

She sighed. She'd done something she had to tell Paul about properly, and Nadia. She couldn't see Morwen's face any more. In a way, she'd done it for Morwen.

She stared at the moon. Silver light all over the city.

She could see, far away, the towers, black silhouettes with bright windows, yellow light streaming out, drawing her towards them. She peeped in. There they were on the trading floors, all men, all young, all active, someone shouting 'Tokyo's come up,' someone else jabbing a finger at a screen, another dialling on a mobile with the landline receiver already at his ear, one of them eating pizza in his cubby-hole office. A crack ran all the way round the top of the block with the noise of thunder, only no-one seemed to notice. She found she could slip in her fingers and hinge the roof slowly back, like the top of a breakfast egg. The sour smell of too many people in one place, of sweat and cheap deodorant rose up round her.

She could see down into the building, right into it, she could see it all so clearly, as if she was there in the room – except she could see other rooms spread out on all sides of her, office beyond office, trading floor beyond trading floor. They were like reflections in the mirrors of a lift, endless, all of them lit up with the glare of strip lights. Everywhere around her there was movement, traders striding between desks, slapping each other's backs, whistling at a secretary as she carried a file through, grabbing at mobile phones, pushing past each other, stuffing burgers in their mouths. There were traders in their shirt-sleeves, traders sitting on the edge of their desks, traders leaning over each other, shouting threats, dropping pills in their coffee, snorting cocaine through fifty-pound notes, one of them handing out bottles of champagne, one of them dialling into a phone-sex line, one of them standing stock-still, staring at the screens, his tie undone, his mouth open – all of them traders, all of them men.

She was somewhere right at the heart of it all, somewhere high up, on the helipad at the top of the Pinnacle, the tallest, newest block in the city, the building that increased the total trading area by ten per cent overnight. She stood there, legs braced, right on the parapet, smelling the wind. Beneath her an abyss stretched down, past countless windows, past seagulls like scraps of paper, past kites and eagles and aeroplanes, into blackness darker than the rivers of hell. She leaned forward into the tempest, her hair streaming out behind her, her arms spread wide, her cheeks icy, her eyes sharper than knife-blades. She stood there, against the sky, staring out over the city, her back straight as a sword, the costume tight on her legs. She felt the force in her body, the power in her shoulders. She sensed the light glinting against a blackness as slick as oil on her cape, on the muscles of her chest and, most of all, on the cowl and mask, dark as a midwinter night. The cowl was so black it seemed to absorb light, her eyes so bright they glowed, commanding, piercing, ruling the city.

She could see all of it, every detail, each of the individual traders, each of the brokers, the back-office people, the programmers, all of them. She could see the assistants making the coffee, serving it out at boardrooms, typing away, welcoming men at reception desks, answering phones, making appointment, making excuses, writing agenda, drafting reports, all of them women, forever smiling, forever dipping their heads, forever patting at their hair, fumbling at their make-up, forever worrying: what did the men think of them? What would the men think of them?

She saw into the computers, she could see the spreadsheets as they lay there: myriad figures jumbled, sorted, shaken, and neatly dropped out, layered, mounting up right to the topmost one, it was the spreadsheet Webster had shown her. She looked at it and through it and behind it, down, down, down, layer and layer to the truth, to the real figures that he kept locked away, for his eyes only, to the figures that were massaged and manipulated and laundered through tax-havens and offshore companies, through Liechtenstein and the Virgin Islands and Jersey and Denver and Hong Kong and Zurich and back again, the figures that no one else must ever see. The truth, the figures that Morwen had groped for through all that modelling and so nearly grasped, the real figures, now there, in front of her, clear as the sky above.

She woke with a jolt. The room was empty. Sunshine streamed through the window. Someone knocked and opened the door. It was Paul, his hair combed down, in a crumpled suit with a tie round his neck and a mug of tea in each hand.

'Good morning, it's a beautiful day!'

'Paul! I have to talk to you.' She sat up, the sun in her eyes. 'Where is everybody?'

'They've gone out. Don't work, don't get paid.'

She put down the mug and seized his hand, pulling him onto the bed beside her. His eyes looked up at her as if she was the only thing in the room and he leaned towards her. She placed a hand each side of his head and held him there with her eyes fixed on his.

'It's about Webster.'

'Bastard.'

'I told you, I stabbed him. I think I killed him.'

'I don't think you did.' He looked at her, his eyes serious, his hands holding onto her wrists: 'One, you ain't a killer. I just know you ain't. Two, I don't see the blood. You stab someone, you're covered in blood. Three, there's nothing on the web. There's stuff about an attack on a city magnate and the police are saying it was a mugging, but that's all. If he was dead, they'd make more fuss.'

'But he lay there making noises. I felt the pen quiver with his heartbeat.'

'Ade,' said Paul, 'He's a bastard, but he's got a pulse. He shuddered or something. And he got what he deserved.'

He was holding her hands in his. She felt better than she had for a long time.

'You're going to be OK,' he said, 'you had a bad time. You just rest here today. We'll look after you.'

She thought of the dream, of the wind in her face, wind that had come a thousand miles over the ocean, over the hills, wind that was pure. He had his head on one side. He looked very young all of a sudden. She leaned towards him.

'I had a pen. I stuck it in his neck and twisted it and I ran and then you came and I had a dream.'

'Tell me later.'

'No, I want to tell you now. Listen.'

She held him there, her mouth next to his ear, smelling the rich unfamiliar scent of the oil in his hair, her fingers on the softness of his skin. She told him everything, about Webster and how he treated Jessica and Sita and the restaurant and the lift and her teeth in his throat. She told him about the streetlights glinting on the tarmac and the alley and how the silk scarf had cut into the fat on Webster's neck, and how she'd hated him and how she'd thought of Morwen. She told him of the pen, sliding effortlessly into the plump flesh, and the blood welling up and how she'd started running.

Then she told him about the dream, how she'd stood there, the dark figure on the Pinnacle leaning on the wind, looking down on it all, watching over it, it had been her and she'd seen into everything, all of it, and grasped it, how it all worked, and it was hers.

When she'd finished she sat back. He gazed at her with his large dark eyes, his mouth open. 'You're something. You need someone to look after you. Stay here. We'll look after you.'

He had such beautiful eyes, the iris amber, the pupil deepest black. She thought: *I'm in control of this.* She squeezed his hand and raised it to her lips, kissing it tenderly, taking her time, keeping her eyes on his.

'You'd better go,' she said. 'I need to think a bit.'

'I'll see you again, won't I?'

'Yeah, see you later.'

He made to kiss her on the lips, hesitated and ducked back. Then he was gone and she lay there thinking, *I'll see him again. Plus I stabbed Webster. I didn't kill him. But he tried to do that to me, so I stabbed him. Bastard.*

13

Ade ran down the escalator, skipped sideways and let three people onto the train in front of her (including two who obviously didn't deserve it.) *Paul Affarn, Paul Affarn ran the rhythm in her head. Paul Affarn. I'll see you again. I'll see you again.* She stopped herself on the platform. *This is crazy,* she thought, *you're a tax inspector, you should not be like this, and it doesn't even rhyme.* Then: *so what? I live in the city. I can be who I want.*

She found herself smiling at a tall woman with magnificent cheekbones and immaculate make-up who ignored her and then poked out a delicate pink tongue. Ade looked back at her, deadpan and, unable to stop herself, broke into a grin. *Paul Affarn, I'll see him again.* The woman looked away. *Point to me,* thought Ade.

She was late for work, there would be so much to do. Everything had gone wrong with Webster. Would they know it was her? Was he really OK? How could they know she'd been there in the alley? But maybe they'd know. They'd ask her when she last saw him, she'd better be ready. They made you tell the story backwards, to trip you up.

A young man in denims carrying chisels and a large hammer and what looked like engraving tools in a dirty hold-all stood up and gave her his seat at Tower Hill.

She stared at her reflection in the blackness. Robin Hood, Robyn Hood, Paul Affarn.

A bright light streaked past. The train slowed and she stood staring at the headline on the free paper in front of her face:

VAMPIRE IN THE CITY! BLOOD-SUCKER SUCKED!

Below it was Webster's face in close-up, heavily bandaged round the neck and cheek, his eyes gleaming in pain and anger.

She jerked back, into the tall woman. 'I'm so sorry,' she began, 'I...'

'Pray think nothing of it,' the woman replied with great attention to consonants, still ignoring her, and swept past.

Ade stood on the escalator at Monument, the wind whipping round her. *Webster's OK*, she thought. Then: *if they're talking about vampires, they don't think it's me. Paul Affarn, I'll see him again. Where did they get the vampire stuff from?*

She was just turning onto the street, when it hit her. She leant against the wall, almost choking with laughter. *I bit the bastard in the neck! Bites in the neck – they think it's a vampire! The bastard hasn't got the guts to tell them what happened in the lift.*

She took a deep breath, then another.

I bit the bastard, she thought, and he ain't going to tell them it was when he tried to rape me. This isn't me. I'm a civil servant. I work with spreadsheets. I have to start taking things seriously.

She pushed through the main entrance on Gracechurch Street and ran up the stairs to the main office. There were people everywhere, mostly men, in suits, holding cups of coffee, making for the other offices in the building. She ducked past and tapped on the keypad for the side door.

'Look out!' someone said in a firm, assertive voice.

She looked back to see a young man with regular features, a cleft chin, his hair brushed back from his forehead, glaring at her and flicking spilled coffee from his fingers.

'Butterfingers!' She slipped through the door and pulled it shut.

Jimmy the Kid, slightly built, a triangular freckled face, vivid blue eyes and red hair, waved the free-sheet at her as she crossed the lobby: 'Seen this! Your Mr Webster's got himself bitten!'

He giggled.

'Thanks. He should check his shadow in the mirror.'

His shadow in the mirror in the lift, the face coming at her, the gross infolding flesh of his neck endlessly reflected away from her. She pushed through the dark wood double doors into the main office.

Most of them were out of their desks, all gathered round Nebay's computer. Nebay who always said she was from Eritrea, full-bodied, tough and loud, who treated the tax office as her family. She was pointing at something on the screen. There was a babble of noise.

Ade let the doors slam. Everyone fell silent, their eyes on her.

'Good morning,' she said. 'Tube was late.'

No-one spoke. No-one said that the Tube wasn't late

for anyone else. She started towards her desk on the far side of the room, next to Denny's office.

'Good morning, Ade,' said Nebay, grinning like she'd won the lottery. 'Terrible news about Mr Webster. He's one of yours, isn't he?'

Ade stopped and looked at her. 'I saw something in the paper. He had an accident. I'm sorry to hear it. Now, we must get on. Lots of public out there.'

'Good job, I say.' This was Joe, sitting on a stool with his mug of tea in his hand. Grade eighteen, no ambitions and a year to his pension. He was always either drinking tea or sucking peppermints. 'Deserved it.'

He looked up at them. 'Only saying what you're all thinking, aren't I?'

'Joe, we treat the public with respect.'

'OK,' said Aidan, stepping away from the doors. 'Let's get organised.' He was in his early thirties and from a large family in Dublin. He was never there a minute after five thirty, but you could rely on him.

Ade took off her coat. They stood there watching her, as she sat down, logged into the computer and started on the morning's emails.

'Ade.'

Denny's voice on the phone. She sounded unhappy. 'Could you come to my office, please?'

There were two people behind the desk this time. The woman was dressed in a dark blue trouser suit, round face, short black hair, dark eyes, and a mouth that seemed to smile even when it wasn't appropriate. Ade felt an immediate sympathy with her. She didn't pay much attention to the man, average height, grey suit, brown hair cut high over his ears and a moustache. Denny was in her usual position for shared interviews, on the hard chair by the window, her face troubled.

Ade put her hands together and found she was clasping her right wrist in her left hand. She smiled at Denny. 'Could you get another chair, Ade?'

'That won't be necessary,' said the man. 'There's no need for you to attend this interview.'

Denny frowned.

'I'm here for the Revenue.'

'That won't be necessary.' He didn't look at her. 'We will conduct the interview.'

'I think I should stay.'

'You've seen our authority.'

Denny got to her feet.

'All right. Ade, may I introduce Inspector Mayland,' she indicated the woman, 'and Sergeant Jones, City of London police force.'

'Chief Inspector,' remarked the woman as if commenting on the weather.

The sergeant followed Denny with his eyes as she moved to the door.

'I'll be outside if you need me.'

He didn't answer. The door closed. He picked up Denny's chair and positioned it in front of the desk.

'Sit down.'

He remained standing.

'Ms Corey,' said the woman. 'Sorry to take up your time. I know you must be very busy. This is about one of your, what do you call them? Tax-payers? Clients?' She smiled. 'Files?'

'Cases.'

'Good. A Mr Rex Webster.'

Ade felt her chest tighten. The Chief Inspector continued. 'Mr Webster was admitted to A and E at St George's in the early hours of this morning. He had been assaulted.'

'How is he?'

Sergeant Jones looked at her sharply.

'He's fine,' said the Chief Inspector. 'Minor injuries to the neck. Quite nasty at the time. Probably frightening.'

Jones cut in. 'Someone stabbed him with a pointed instrument in the fleshy part of the neck.' He shot out a long arm and tapped Ade on the back of the neck before she could jerk back. It felt like a peck. 'Just there. And a bite wound to the throat. Superficial. He doesn't really remember what happened.'

'That's what started off all this nonsense about vampires,' said Mayland. 'Now all the no-hopers have joined in. Copy-cats. Selfies of time-wasters with vampire-teeth, ghouls chasing businessmen everywhere on Facebook. It's a carnival out there.'

She smiled and Ade warmed to her. She continued: 'Fun, but we won't allow it. Affects the overseas trade. Nip it in the bud. The City needs stability and security.'

She paused

'You've got to ask yourself,' said Jones, 'was it an amateur? Some kind of crime passionelle?' He pronounced it to rhyme with "jelly". 'Was it revenge or a warning? Or maybe it was a publicity stunt. It's the kind of thing that gets a lot of attention on the net.'

Ade said nothing. Jones slipped out a newspaper he'd

been carrying folded under his arm, a tabloid. Eighty-point headlines screamed: 'CITY BLOOD-SUCKER' Superimposed in one corner was the photo of Webster, his eyes glaring, bandages wrapped round his neck and scalp, his cheeks showing bruises.

Ade felt the laughter surging up within her. *I must not laugh*, she thought. She rammed a fist in her mouth and snorted. Jones stared at her. 'That your reaction? You think it's funny? Some people do.' Mayland looked at her like she was passing judgement.

Ade breathed out carefully. 'I'm sorry, but it's the headline. Some economists do see city brokers as essentially parasitic on the productive sectors of the economy.'

I said that so fluently, she thought.

'You can argue about that at your university. Please read it, out loud.'

'Pardon?'

'Best to cooperate,' said Mayland. 'Indulge us.'

Ade picked up the paper. 'Vampires Stalk City Streets.' She glanced up at them and continued, keeping her voice level. 'Respected businessman Mr Rex Webster, 58, was attacked near Tooley Street on his way home from a business meeting. The attacker, who has not been identified, inflicted wounds to his neck, including a bite. He was admitted to St George's Hospital and then transferred to the Consultancy Clinic. He was later allowed home.'

Jones held up a hand. 'That's enough. There's a lot more about urban vampires and copycat attacks and Occupy St Pauls and the 99 per cent. Did the City a lot of damage, that lot. The City is the world's leading business centre. We cannot afford more trouble.'

'Now,' Mayland consulted the file in front of her, 'We understand from Mr Webster's accountant that you had a meeting yesterday afternoon and that Mr Webster took you to dinner.'

Ade nodded.

'Was that normal?'

'Not exactly. We seek to confine our relationship with cases to professional matters. However, I had been encouraged to be more cordial in this case – business-friendly, it's called. The instructions came from the Minister. I'm sure his office will confirm.'

Keep it serious, she thought. *You're doing well.*

'We understand that you left the restaurant separately.'

'Yes.'

'It wasn't a question; we have information on your movements. Where did you go?'

Ade kept her eyes fixed on Mayland's. 'Where did I go? I walked about for a bit, then I visited a friend.'

Jones glanced at Mayland. She ignored him.

'An old friend or a new friend?'

'I met him quite recently.'

'His name?'

'Mr Paul Affarn.'

'Exactly.' Mayland smiled, her forehead wrinkling sympathetically. 'It's not for me to give you advice, but you should be careful whom you associate with.' She put a slight emphasis on the 'm' of whom.

'I agree,' said Ade. 'Not for you.' *Did I say that?*

She folded her arms. Mayland nodded to the sergeant.

'Tell Ms Corey what we have on Mr Paul Affarn.'

Jones opened a notebook and read in a formal voice,

like a school-boy in class: 'Mr Paul Conroy a.k.a. Speedy Paul a.k.a. Paul Affarn born Brick Lane 1993, degree course in social work, Greenwich University, 2014, left without a qualification, six months unattached youth work Tower Hamlets, left when non-statutory services shut down, worked for Centrepoint, CRISIS, Haringey against Homelessness, short term contracts. Believed associated with Occupy, active in Occupation of St Pauls, arrests for vagrancy, incitement to public disorder, theft, aggravated disorder.'

Jones stared at Ade and continued: 'He was in the Harrods riot, said he was trying to calm things down, but the magistrates didn't believe him. Three months. Multiple arrests for residential trespass – that's squatting to you. He's a ring-leader, likes to make trouble. That kind of lad. We'll get him properly one day.'

Mayland ignored him. 'So you went visiting Mr Affarn?'

'Yes. There were at least ten witnesses there.'

'I'm sure there were. Mr Affarn is a squatter I believe. No fixed address. Weakens credibility in court.' She looked seriously at Ade. 'You really should be more careful about your friends.'

She held up a hand

'I know. None of my business.'

She scratched at her ear.

'Back to Mr Webster. I want you to think carefully before you answer, Ms Corey. Mr Webster was just a case to you? You can't think of anyone who would wish to assault him?'

'No. He may have made enemies in business, but I just

dealt with his tax accounts. We approved them yesterday. The case is now resolved.' Ade looked at Jones, then Mayland. 'May I go?'

'You're sure you have nothing to tell us about Webster?'

'I'm sorry I can't tell you anything.' *Except he's a bastard,* she thought.

'We may need to talk to you again. Don't go away. And don't talk to anyone about this. That means: do not talk to anyone about anything to do with this case.'

Mayland sighed. 'I had hoped to clear this up today. Come on, Jeremy. Legwork.'

Jones grunted, nodded at Ade and moved to the door. Mayland beat him to the handle, held the door open and waved him through. She glanced back at Ade. Ade felt that she was appraising her, and that she couldn't quite make up her mind.

14

The office door opened and Denny came in.

'Don't go, Ade, we'd better have a chat.'

She crossed to the desk and sat in her chair, leaning back, her eyes closed. She's been in this job a long time, thought Ade. The outer office was completely quiet.

Ade wished Morwen was with her, that it was like it had been when they'd started, when the models and the spreadsheets were just an idea that the rest of the office made jokes about and they talked over in coffee-breaks, with doughnuts if it was going well. Denny had approved the project and given them time to develop it. None of the others ever mentioned Morwen now, only Denny.

Denny opened her eyes and leaned forward, her elbows on the desk. 'Webster paid up: your original assessment, first thing this morning. Didn't argue about it, just wired the money. Biggest single item this office has ever taken. You've done well. Very well.'

'Wow!' Ade stared at her. *I should be delighted. I hate him.* 'I don't know what to say.'

'Something's scared him. And there's this city vampire business. Some of the others are paying up too. And there's the visit from the Special Advisor. And cops in the office. Something happened.'

'I'm sorry, Denny. I just wanted the thing to work.'

'Denny? Is that what they call me? I didn't know.' Denny seemed to be thinking about it. 'Better than Denise any day. I always hated Denise at school.'

'I settled the Webster account yesterday afternoon, before all this happened. If that's any help.'

Denny didn't seem to be listening to her. 'Mayland and Jones are City of London. Richest patch in Europe. Biggest Fraud Division. Lowest clear-up rate. They don't investigate fraud, they license it. They're trouble. It was City of London that came for Morwen.' She paused for a moment. 'What are they doing, coming here about a minor assault which isn't anything to do with us?'

'I'm sorry.'

'I'm on your side,' said Denny. 'You know that don't you?'

If you stared long enough you could just make out the bricks in the wall behind her. Ade thought of the wall in the alleyway, the cardboard boxes stacked against it.

'There was a problem.' She felt she was choking. *He tried to rape me. Should I say that? Who would believe me? Am I going to be the one who got raped, is that how they'll know me, any office I go to?* 'I handled it.'

Denny nodded slowly. 'Perhaps it's best I don't know.' She paused again, her brown eyes fixed on Ade's.

'They're bastards, they think they own everything.' Ade tried to smile at her, but she felt something pricking in the corner of her eye. She kept her voice flat.

'I followed the rules, business-friendly, like that advisor said. The office has taken more tax in a morning than it usually does in a month. It's really down to

Morwen's model. The government's desperate to cut the deficit. You'll be a hero.'

'Maybe. I'd like to think it worked like that.'

Denny reached across the table and put her hand on Ade's then slid it back. 'You have to watch out for the City of London lot. They're poison. Just remember you've done better than anyone in this office. And take a week off. Discretionary leave. You've been working very hard. Anyone else I'd have said too hard. You deserve a rest and you need one.'

She stared down at her hand on the desk and at Ade's. 'Anything I can do, just ask.'

'Thanks. It's OK. I handled it.'

Ade closed the door to Denny's room behind her and turned round to face the office. Nebay was rushing towards her down the aisle between the desks. 'She's here. Congratulations!'

They were all on their feet clapping her. Nebay made a whooping sound and flung her arms round her. Ade gently disentangled herself.

'Thanks, but it's just my job.'

Aidan stepped forward: 'Biggest tax take of anyone in the history of the office. That's a real achievement, Ade. We all want to congratulate you.'

She shook his hand then Joe's then the others, and finally Jimmy the Kid's. She swallowed. 'Just everyone remember: it's really all down to the Model, Morwen's model.'

No-one spoke. She found she couldn't look at them. Then Nebay turned round from something she'd been doing at her desk and shouted: 'Cake all round.'

She had the double-chocolate sponge already cut into big slices, the cream spilling out thick onto the paper napkins. She offered the biggest slice to Ade.

'Gosh, this is wonderful. Let me sit down.' She took a bite of the sugary mixture then crammed it into her mouth. She remembered Morwen in the coffee shop with the pain aux raisins. The coarse sweetness flooded her senses. 'That's some cake,' she said.

'Went out for it as soon as we heard. And there's squirty cream.'

'Thank you,' said Ade, 'Thank you so much. You're a great team, it's really good to have your support.'

She looked round at them. And Morwen, she thought. Morwen did this.

She stood on the pavement looking down the street. A steady rain was falling. It was dark, but not four o'clock yet. She'd never left the office before 6.30. Crowds of people were streaming towards her. A business man in a trilby and a black raincoat shoved past and she moved back so he didn't step on her toes. He was followed by a group of office workers chattering noisily, their umbrellas jostling each other and dripping on all sides. She pushed her way into the flow. Everyone ignored her.

The shop at the corner was doing good business. She took a diet coke out of the fridge. The assistant leaned over the counter and looked at the money she'd put down.

'Cheers,' he grunted, raising soft brown eyes. 'Take care of yourself.'

'Sorry?'

'I know you. You been coming here every day for

two years. You've never been this early and you look … different.'

'Oh, thank you. No, it's just… I got a dental appointment.'

'Ah,' he said. 'Good luck.'

He picked up the money carefully.

She poured the saccharin drink into her mouth. The exhilaration swept through her again. *The city vampire. Bad for business, good for taxes. Someone's on our side. And I bit that bastard. And Paul knew I wasn't a murderer.*

She thought of the pen sliding slick into the flesh. Once it had punctured the skin, it seemed to require no effort at all, as if it was someone else doing it and she was just watching. She shook her head and walked rapidly to the station.

Suddenly there was a crackle of noise echoing off the buildings around her and a great crest of fireworks reached up, spreading out across the sky. Silver stars fanned out, tumbling slowly back to earth. More and more of them, further away across the city. *And I'm going to see him again. Paul Affarn. I'll see him again. And I'm carrying a stack of cash I don't know what to do with.* She looked up at the stars and at the black sky behind them. She couldn't help laughing. The newsagent stood in the doorway of his shop, staring after her.

15

Ade breathed in the smell: burgers, chips, ketchup. She loved it. She was sitting in the corner against the window in her favourite café, in Whitechapel, just up the road from her flat in Sydney Street. She had on her best jeans and fleece jacket and the lime green ankle-boots.

People from the city were all around her: workers catching something to eat on the way home, people who wanted something quick before going to the movies, locals who couldn't be bothered to cook, none of them thinking about vampires. A family with two children was at the next table, laughing as the mother, a short blond-haired woman, opened her eyes wide and told the children she was going to magic their burgers into monkey-burgers – you had to look for the tails. Ade could see she had peanuts hidden in her other hand under the table. A hubbub of conversation rose up on all sides. No-one paid Ade any attention at all, but she kept the seat opposite her free.

A slight dark figure entered and stood by the door looking round. Paul. She knew him before she saw his face. She felt the blood pulsing in her throat. Why am I feeling like this? Today, after everything? Because I can be who I want to be. She half-rose and waved. He smiled at her and moved gracefully between the tables. He was still wearing the suit but his tie was loose and his hair ruffled. He leaned forward, took her hand and kissed her on the lips. He tasted of lollipops.

'It's really good to see you again,' she said as he slid into the seat opposite.

'You're here. I knew you'd be here.'

''Course I'm here, it's my favourite café. Do you like it?'

'Wait til I've eaten something. What do they do that's veggie?'

'Ah… eggs? Beans? We can go somewhere else.' She reached for her coat.

'No, I want to try it.'

He looked up at her from under the curly black hair. A young woman in a blue overall came up and took their order: burgers, chips and coke.

'I've been happy all day,' he said. He looked even younger when he smiled.

'Me too.'

'Actually it's been a terrible day. I didn't want to tell you last night, 'cos you had enough. But we had the meeting with the Council about the Homeless Centre grant today.'

The suit! That was why he was wearing a suit this morning. And he'd had his hair trimmed.

'Oh Paul, I wish I'd known. Did you get it?'

'No, course not, they've cut everything. But I've got a lottery ticket.' He held it up and the smile was back. She stared at him.

'You do the lottery? But it's rubbish. You stand more chance of squatting being legalised.'

'If I win, that funds the Centre. Then I can really do something for Johnno and Nadia and Casey and all of them. Organise. Get them their rights. I'm going to do it. Somehow I'll get the money.'

'Sure.' She grimaced. 'Actually, I've had a weird day. Everything went crazy.'

'Tell me about it.'

So she did.

'That's cool,' he said. 'That's so cool. Not the bit about the cops, but the tax and your boss and the rest of it.'

He felt in his pocket. 'Something to show you.'

He placed a pile of cards on the table and leaned forward to fan then out. She loved his hair, the rich smell of an oil she didn't recognise.

'Mariska helped. She knows someone who does printing.'

His eyes were on hers, his face ready to smile.

The cards were identical: the silhouette of a woman, caped, in a tight-fitting costume against a full moon, a logo in the corner, and writing in gothic script.

'They're business cards,' she said. 'Who are they for? And who's this? A super-hero?'

'It's you. Read what it says: it's *Tax Woman – Champion of the Welfare State.*' He couldn't help grinning, proud as the dog that brought back the stick.

'I'd never fit into the costume. And I can't do press-ups.'

'Look at it properly. She's a real woman. She isn't as thin as a rake, she's tall and she stands like everyone else and she's not sucking her stomach in and poking her chest out. And she's got normal muscles and – look – she's carrying a brief-case. She's lovely,' he said. 'She's like you.'

He paused and waited.

'That's me?'

'Certainly is.' His eyes sparkled. 'You're Tax Woman. Number one.'

'What – you mean I safeguard the city by night and strike fear into the hearts of tax-dodgers everywhere? It's not like that. Wish it was. It's mostly spreadsheets.'

'Don't matter. When you told me your dream, I knew. I could see you there, looking out, watching over the city, all of them, the grabbers and the givers, the rich and the poor. It's how I see you. I can't help it.'

He looked up at her with his gentle eyes and she felt a rush of feeling for him. *Why not? Just for once, do what you want to do and don't listen to the bit that says 'Let's just think about this.'*

Why ever not?

She seized his hand. 'OK. And you can be part of it. We're a team!'

She pulled him towards her across the table and kissed him, full on the mouth. She felt his arms tight round her. *If I could stop time now, just now, us together like this, in front of everyone, not caring about anything, that would be … number one.*

Someone coughed next to her. 'Double burger and beans twice, one real, one veggie, one chips, two coke, one diet.'

The young woman slapped the two plates down on the table. She was about eighteen, freckled, with fine fair hair and pallid, slightly greasy skin. There was a burn mark on her wrist. She stared incuriously at them, caught Ade's eye, winked and turned away.

'The two of us,' said Ade. 'We don't fight crime. We make the thing work. I'm tax and you're spend. I help get the money in, you run the Centre, supporting people who need it. But it's not going to be easy.'

'You're cool. You can make a difference, like I said: you're number one.'

She looked at him. *He really believes it.*

'I nearly killed Webster. I hate him.'

'You got issues. All heroes have issues. Makes you stronger. If you'd just gone home after the restaurant, licked your wounds, nothing would have happened.' *And I wouldn't have met you again*, she thought. *And there's the wad of cash, snug in my pocket.*

Paul stared at her across the table. 'It's cool.' He grinned, then frowned.

'What's the problem?' she said.

'Nothing.'

'You should tell me. It's no good if we don't tell each other things.'

'OK,' he looked away, then back at her, his eyes serious. 'It's just… I thought of something. The black buddy.'

'Don't you understand? You've seen the movies. The black buddy.'

She looked at him.

'The black buddy,' he said 'always takes the bullet in the final scene. For Whitey. Whitey's fine, everyone's sorry for black buddy. I'm the black buddy.'

His eyes gleamed. 'It's OK,' he said. 'I can dodge.'

'Don't worry. It's not going to be that kind of movie. We're writing the script.'

'Sure. It's just… forget it. We got to think about a transport, a long low black car, with ejector seats and afterburners. And gadgets.'

'Push-bikes. Better for the environment.' A voice in her said: *Trust your feelings.*

She reached inside her jacket. 'And I got something for the Centre. Get us started.'

She pulled the envelope out of her pocket and laid it on the table between them, the wad of money showing at the torn end. Paul stared at it and then at her.

'Cool,' he said, very softly.

16

They were in the pub, warm and safe, with condensation on the windows and the comfortable feeling she always had in a pub, and dark brown woodwork and beautiful gleaming brass.

'Have another one,' she said, 'we should celebrate,' and pointed at his glass, missing it. *Jesus*, she thought, *this is going to be a night. We should be making plans about Robyn Hood, but we can do that later.*

'Watch it,' said Paul, 'You'll get pissed.'

'You ain't seen me drink. Not properly.'

She put her hand against the wall to steady herself and dived into the crowd round the bar. *Best pub in Bethnal Green. No one ever hassles you, everyone friendly. Never been here before. Show 'em how I can drink.*

She was laughing at something when she got back to him, but she couldn't remember what it was. He seemed to think it was funny too.

'Whisky chasers,' she said, 'doubles. Down in one.'

They were on the street and she couldn't remember how they got there. Rain pattered on her face. She reached out and felt the drops on her palm, on the back of her hand. So soft, so gentle, like a butterfly walking on her skin.

Paul grabbed her arm and stumbled against her. 'Come on,' he said. 'We're lost.'

She pushed at him. He was soft too, soft and gentle, like a big Wobbly Joe. You pushed at him, he went away, and he came back. You pushed at him again, he came back again.

'You are pissed.' He started laughing again. 'Why do you keep pushing me?'

'Course I am. So are you!'

She had him clasped tight against her now so they could both walk together, from streetlight to streetlight, into shadow, into light, into shadow, into light. There must be an all-night bus somewhere, she was sure there was. She was off work, she could take him back with her, she didn't have to get up tomorrow, they could lie there all morning ... *Don't think about it.*

She heard the rumble of an engine and a glowing shape, all windows with rain on them and yellow light loomed up out of the darkness. She pushed Paul and he stuck out his arm, swaying towards it, suddenly bright in the head-lights.

A horn blared out and she held her ears and it was sweeping past them, on and off into the night.

'Missed it,' he said. 'We need a bus-stop. Let's keep walking.'

'Maybe there's a café. There's always a café.'

They were somewhere else, there weren't any pubs. There were tall concrete buildings all around them, white and faintly luminous in the moonlight. She couldn't see anyone on the streets. Paul had gone quiet. He was concentrating on walking, holding onto her hand, guiding her along, keeping just on the edge of the path. She wanted to sit down.

'Got a cigarette?' she said.

'Don't smoke, gave it up. So did you. You said.'

'Yeah. Mostly. Let's get another drink.'

There was a burst of noise, a babble of talking and the rattle of glasses, abruptly cut off. A group of men were standing on the pavement right in front of them outside an entrance with steps. She could see the glow of cigarettes.

'Come on,' she said.

One of the men was looking at her. He was large, broad-faced, with fat round his eyes and a barrel-chest. A fedora hat was pushed back on his head. The image of a laughing village bobby flashed into Ade's mind.

'Whoa,' he said, holding up a large hand. 'It's a private showing. Where's your invitation?'

'Don't be mean, Ronnie,' said one of the others. 'You can let her in. It's your gallery. Don't know about her friend though.'

He sniggered.

'She big enough for you, Ronnie?' one of them said.

Everyone was laughing, even Paul.

Ade had Paul by the arm. 'Come on, you can't leave him out in the cold. Show us your gallery.'

They were all laughing, gathering behind her, pushing her forward.

Then they were in a bright room with pictures on the walls and people standing in ones and twos looking at them. *It's an art gallery. Mum loved art. She knew nothing about it, but she loved it. She'd never been in a gallery – or maybe she had, before I was born. Dear Mum!*

The clothes they were wearing would cost a fortune. She was out of place, but who cares? It's art. She knew she'd seen some of the people before, but she couldn't think where.

Ronnie looked out of place too. His clothes were probably expensive but they didn't look smart on him, his gut bulging over his waistband. His expression was wrong too, the cheerful smile of someone pleased with himself who wanted to share his feelings, not the elegant closed faces and appraising eyes of the others. She looked round the room and a thought bobbed up in her mind: they're all here because they think they can get something out of it. Not Ronnie, he just likes the occasion.

There were tables with wine bottles on them at the corners of the room and someone holding out a glass, brimful. Ade downed the wine, the bubbles tickling her throat. She knew she didn't belong here, but it was good booze. Another one and they'd move on. Paul grinned at her, a glass in each hand. She looked round. No one seemed to be enjoying the pictures, no one was even smiling. A woman in blue jeans and an elegantly cut crimson T-shirt next to her pointed at a delicate water-colour of the Windscale Plant: 'Three hundred thousand! Saw one just like that go for a hundred in Amsterdam last week. Same artist. Euros.'

Her partner, a younger man with impossibly smooth skin in a neat business suit, paused in front of a giant crucifixion, a collage of thousands of ATM receipts. He wrinkled his nose: 'Two forty-seven for this! Ronnie's pushing his luck. He's lost it.'

She felt a pressure in the small of her back and took

a pace forward. Ronnie was standing next to her, moving her gently forward, like he owned her and was showing her off.

'Pictures,' said Ronnie. She could feel his breath, warm and moist on her cheek. 'I love 'em. I love art, all of it, modern, old, avant garde, retro, it's so exciting. I love it. Good investment, too – never pay any tax on it, the way I do it, neither do my friends,' he winked. 'I got friends, lots of friends. See the one I just bought?'

He pointed: a black canvas with a streak of lightning, jagged, brilliant white, searing across it and a scale in percentage of GDP up the left hand edge. The label said "Flashback". When Ade looked closely she saw the black was made up of an infinite number of shades of dark grey, drab green, navy blue, so that it seemed to waver and recede in front of her and she felt sick and couldn't really focus on it.

'Very nice,' she said. She had a glass in each hand now. She raised one of them to Paul.

'Yes, got 'em all at home, Tintoretto, Hockney, some my five-year old did.'

He gave a bark of laughter, then looked at her appraisingly and ran his hand across his mouth. 'You like art? You should come and see them.'

'I don't think so.'

'Put lots of money in this gallery. Buy and sell, buy and sell – but only to people with too much money, that's the secret. Put half a million pounds over your fire-place, that's money. They all know me here. They love pictures, sure they do. They think they're a good investment. They love money.'

Those people. She'd seen them before in their business suits the other side of polished oak desks, at Somerset House in front of the Tribunal, one of them walking down the street in front of her once, chatting to the permanent secretary. She glanced round. They were here, everywhere, all of them, the men from the city, the bastards who sneered at her across the desk and never paid up. She felt instantly on her guard. None of them recognised her, she was alright with Ronnie. *Where was Paul? We should leave soon, soon as I've finished my drink.*

Ronnie raised his hand to a crop-haired young woman with the face of a china doll and shrewd grey eyes. She wore a tight silvery dress and sat perched on the edge of the drinks table. She nodded to him, hardly moving her head, and continued to survey the room.

He was laughing. 'Artists! Hey, Annie, what do you think of my latest?'

He touched the painting. The young woman glanced swiftly at it.

'Chip-paper.'

'Don't be like that. It's art.'

He rested a hand on the woman's shoulder. She jerked away from him, turned and ran her eyes over Ade as if she were a dress she couldn't make up her mind about. Ade felt the blood rushing to her face.

'Don't think much of your other latest, either.'

She stared at the woman. Ronnie nudged her.

'See. Temperamental. But they're artists. All my friends are artists. Don't take it to heart. Come on Annie, give me your professional opinion.'

The woman laughed: 'I'm not bidding, not my oyster,

and there's so much competition around these days. Paintings, you know where you are, but… maybe ten, maybe twenty.'

Ade took a pace towards her, slopping wine out of the glass. 'Show some respect. I'm not for sale.'

'You should ask him what he thinks, dearie.' The woman nodded at Ronnie and stalked away.

'Don't take any notice of her. She's upset, she did the Windscale one. Hasn't sold.' He stood back and studied Ade, his eyes running down her body. Ade felt suddenly anxious. She looked round for Paul. He was filling his glass at the next table.

'I've got to go,' she said.

'Just a minute.' The fat man was holding her by the arm just above the elbow. 'You're worth a lot more than she thinks. Don't be upset. You could take up modelling. I can help. I'm somebody in this world, you know.'

He let go of her arm. There was an appeal in his eyes; he wanted people to like him, he wanted to show off to them. She could see them all around the room, drinking his wine and carefully avoiding him, and sneering at him to each other.

He chuckled, he sounded pleased with himself. 'I'm serious. Hey, Grant.'

He waved to a sharp-faced man in a three-piece suit who reminded Ade of a younger Sergeant Jones, without the moustache. Improvement.

The man glanced at him, mumbled 'Excuse me,' and pushed past.

Ronnie raised his voice: 'Grant. I want your advice.'

'Yes, Mr Wells. How can I help?'

'This young man is Grant Forniss,' said Ronnie to Ade. 'One of my employees. He'll go far.'

Grant didn't bother to hide his frown. 'I'm an intern, Mr Wells, an associate. I was just checking on the guests.'

'Well here's one you should be polite to. Annie thinks she's worth a lot more than my picture. What do you say?'

The young man tilted his head on one side and ran his eyes down Ade's body. She suddenly felt everyone was looking at her as if she had a price tag round her neck. She couldn't see where Paul had gone.

'I say, Annie always was an optimist. I have to go.'

The fat man laughed happily.

'I have to go too,' said Ade. She stepped forward, caught her foot against the table and swayed sideways, slopping most of the drink out of her glass.

'Here, enjoy yourself, have another before you go.' He winked again. None of the rich people were looking at them. She thought she caught sight of Webster with a silk cravat round his neck, at the centre of a group of people, but he was turning away, she couldn't be sure.

'I've got my own supply. Art and booze, booze and art. Nothing better.'

He's not like Webster, arrogant with his wealth, he's vulnerable, he wants people to be his friends. He likes art, just like Mum did. Her thoughts came slow, like treacle. She wanted another drink. The air in the room was heavy and close. The fat man was busy at a side-table. He passed her a large bowl-shaped glass full of sparkling pink wine.

'This is the stuff.'

The drink tasted sharp and rich at the same time. She took another sip. Everything round her suddenly became clearer. She stared across the room. The person she'd thought was Webster had gone.

The fat man was standing very close to her, drinking something that looked like water but smelled pure. He kept glancing over her shoulder to see who else was around.

'Between you and me, you shouldn't take much notice of 'em. Artists, all jealous as hell. I dabble, and then it's business of course. But I love the art.' He took another swig out of his glass. 'There's always business. Everyone in the city wants pictures, investment, that's all they care about. Money eh? Buy and sell and never tell the taxman. You've got to live.'

His eyes sparkled. 'We're different, you and me. We know how to enjoy ourselves.'

Ade felt dizzy. She wanted to find something to say to make him go away for a minute. He was standing too close to her. She made a motion with her hand and he seized it to steady her. She felt his other hand brush against her back and slide down across her bottom. She didn't want him to do that. She put out her other hand and rested it on the edge of the table. Everything in the room seemed very near and jumbled together and far away at the same time.

She heard Wells saying, 'You're good fun. Just hang on here. I'll get us a taxi.'

She didn't want him to get a taxi. Then Paul was next to her. She clutched at his arm.

'You don't look too good,' he was saying. 'Let's go,' and she was cold and he was wrapping a quilted coat she'd never seen before round her.

It was dark and they were on the street and he was there, guiding her along. She felt dizzy again. She started thinking about the rhythm of the streetlights, into shadow, into brightness, into shadow, trying to match her steps to the lights so she could stride between them.

'Careful, girl,' said Paul. 'Hold onto my arm.'

Someone was calling after them. 'Hi! Don't go! I've got a taxi.'

She heard a car engine start up. Headlights swung round, across her and Paul. The taxi slid into her field of vision and stopped just in front of her with its door open. She took a pace back. The fat man, Ronnie, was there, very near her. Then Paul was right in front of her, jabbing his finger at Ronnie.

'Get back to your gallery. Nothing for you here.'

The fat man grinned at him. 'Don't be like that.' He reached out to put an arm round Paul's shoulder.

'Get lost.'

Paul shoved at him with both hands but Ronnie just stood there with the grin across his face, like they were playing a game. She felt dizzy. She needed someone to lean on. She didn't like Ronnie. She started to move forward.

The streetlights were glaring down on her, and suddenly she was in the darkness between them and she couldn't find Paul. The drink tasted sour in her mouth. Everything went quiet and then there was a movement in the shadow beyond the circle of light and someone was lurching out at her, she couldn't make out a face, just a figure in a hoodie with writing across his chest.

'Fucking gimme,' the man grunted. He had his hand out as if he wanted to give her something, something that glinted in the streetlight.

'Vinny! I know you.'

It was Paul's voice. Paul must have moved very fast, he'd got there, in front of her. She wanted to see what the man had in his hand, but she couldn't because Paul was in the way.

'You don't want to be doing this, Vinny.' Paul was pronouncing the words with great care as if everything depended on how he said them. 'You don't want to do this.'

She could hear the taxi revving its engine slowly as it followed them along the street, its door still open. Paul spread his arms out wide, his hands open to show there was nothing in them.

'Kinhell. It's Paul,' said the man in the hoodie. 'You shouldn't be here. What you doing here?'

The fat man said something behind her and he was laughing very loud, as loud as the taxi engine. Vinny, the one in the hoodie, dropped something that clattered on the pavement. He threw his arms round Paul.

'Me mate,' he said indistinctly.

''S OK, Vinny. But I got to go now. I'll catch you later. On the street.'

The fat man had her by the arm and he wouldn't let her go. She said something to him and it must have been funny because he giggled and put his arm right round her.

Then she was in the taxi with him and his face seemed enormous, looming over her, round like the moon, and she couldn't see Paul anywhere and the engine was roaring louder and louder and the streetlights hurtled past, bright, dark, bright, dark, bright, dark.

She was in a lift staring into the mirror, at her face, at the reflection: infinite faces staring into infinite faces, stretching off and fading slowly into a blur. There were fumes rising all round her in an intricate pattern. They smelt as rich as incense. If she could solve the maze everything would be all right.

Ronnie was next to her, and he had his hands on her, pulling at her. Paul wasn't there. She wanted him to be there. She felt Ronnie's face pressed down on her, she smelled the most exquisite cologne. For an instant it was overpowering. She felt she was going to faint. He isn't a bad man, she thought, is he? He wants to be an artist, and they won't let him, they're all laughing at him.

17

She was in a flat she didn't recognise, in a small bathroom, staring into another mirror. It took her a moment to recognise herself. She drank a glass of water, straight down, cold as melting snow in her throat, then another, then another. She was still thirsty. She looked around her. Everything neat, everything orderly. The rows of neat little jars in the cupboard, each labelled with a letter in italics in alphabet order: pills, capsules, powder, granules. She didn't have the faintest idea what they were. She felt uneasy and closed the cupboard door without making any noise.

She realised she didn't need the light on, it was dawn outside. She listened. At first there was just a car starting in the next street, then she caught it: birdsong, a blackbird just outside the window, loveliest of songbirds, you hardly ever heard them in the city.

She pressed down on the door-handle. The sight of the room and that rich incense smell brought everything back. He'd stood there, in the middle of the Arab-patterned carpet, pointing to the pictures on the walls. He'd been talking about them, how much he loved them, how he wished he could do something like that, just once, how much they were worth. He kept talking about how people bought them, a present for someone who's done you a favour – word of mouth, no paper, so the tax man doesn't know – and he suddenly looked sly. *He's not horrible, but he's a bastard,* she thought.

There was a Hockney, he'd said it was very early, and a genuine Tintoretto, postcard sized, a cartoon, in an ormolu frame. There were sculptures, including one that looked very much like a Degas dancer, a copy he'd said. There was a long sofa, velvety, the cushions all in a heap at one end, the velvet smooth and warm on the skin, soft as silk, the seam that pressed into your back, one of the cushions slightly torn where they'd...oh my god!

She stood, not moving for some minutes. She felt the anger inside her growing, spreading out and filling her. The jars in the bathroom and that drink he'd given her that made everything crystal clear and distant all at once, and then she'd felt dizzy and the roar of the taxi engine filled her mind, and there were the mirrors in the lift with her face and his face endlessly curving away from her, and Paul wasn't there, there was only Ronnie's face, large and round and sallow, filling up her whole vision, and he was laughing, his genial, all-embracing, overpowering laugh.

She moved noiselessly forward and touched the sofa, then ran her fingers along it, very gently, lifted them and smelled the tips. She stood there, looking round, not moving. She thought of the sofa, but no images would come. She smelled at the air in the room and she hated him, with a cold, methodical hatred.

The door to the bedroom stood open. She could see his naked feet poking out from the sheets over the end of the bed, plump, the toes curled round. He was snoring softly. He'd done that to her, he'd used her like they always used her, those men who ruled money. It wasn't sex, it wasn't pleasure, it was power, and now he was asleep and she could do anything she wanted. She picked up one of the cushions and pressed it against her face, smelling it, his odour. Then she pushed it away and breathed in deeply, cool, clean air.

She gripped the cushion between both hands and moved slowly to the bedroom door. He was lying prone, rounded, overweight, naked, pink, the dimples below his buttocks and under his shoulder muscles prominent. His head was on the pillow, turned sideways, his mouth wide open, his neck creased.

She thought of the sofa but again no images came. There was strength in that fat body, she knew that. She thought of the pen, sliding into Webster's fat neck with no resistance at all. She thought of the gallery, Ronnie's hand on her back, like he owned her, like he was exhibiting her, of the way he took her arm in the street, of the way he got his arms round and half pulled, half led her into his flat. She tightened her grip on the cushion and advanced towards the bed.

The fat man let out a sigh, farted, and shifted slightly. He looked like a huge bloated baby. She thought of Morwen. She thought of Paul somewhere out on the street, of his face when he leaned forward over the table in the café, of the way he said 'All heroes have issues.' *It's what you do about them that counts,* she thought. She put the cushion down, very carefully, and moved back into the sitting room.

She looked round, trying to collect her thoughts. The Tintoretto (very small) and the Hockney were too obvious.

Blek Le Rat? Rita Ackermann – that wasn't too large? She lifted them down, one by one, and laid them carefully against the sofa. Then she went back into the bedroom. He hadn't moved. She picked up a sheet from the floor and carried it back and spread it out. What the hell, quality counts. She took the Tintoretto and the Ackermann and wrapped it round them. Not just fifty-pound notes. These were real money.

Light was streaming into the room now. The wallet was on a side table. She flipped it open, pulled out the thick wad of notes and slid it into her jacket pocket beside the envelope. She stood there, thinking. Outside the window the blackbird sang to the sun.

She caught an aromatic odour, like lighter fluid. She followed it behind a curtain into an alcove. An expensive draughtsman's board was set up at an angle to catch the light from the window. There was a sheet of cartridge paper clipped to it, with a half-completed pencil sketch of a young man, naked, mimicking the pose of Michelangelo's David, a sneer on his face. She recognised him, the sharp-faced young man from the gallery last night. On the card table lay a mess of parti-coloured rags and paint-brushes and some tubes of paint and oil.

'He dabbles,' she thought. 'He's a bastard and he dabbles.'

She stood on the pavement, looking up and down the road. The sunlight hurt her eyes. She walked smartly away from the entrance to the flats, her gaze fixed straight ahead.

Paul was walking beside her.

'I waited. He came up in the taxi and I had to sort

Vinny out and he grabbed at you. He was too quick and I couldn't stop him. I ran after the taxi and I couldn't catch it but I kept running and I saw where you went. It was a heck of a long way.'

'I waited.' He wasn't looking at her. He had his hands jammed down in his pockets. 'It was cold.'

'Sorry. I'm very sorry. Last night. I was a bit pissed.'

'Just a bit. So was I. I was hammered.'

She shifted the pictures under her arm and took his hand. Then she halted and put her arm round him and pressed her body hard against him. His head was down, forced into her shoulder. She caressed the soft curly hair at the nape of his neck.

'I'm so sorry,' she said. 'Thanks for waiting.'

'S'not a problem.' He didn't look up at her.

She gripped his hand tightly then linked her fingers between his. *Why am I apologising? I shouldn't be saying sorry, it's not me that did something wrong. He did that to me, and he will pay.*

'It's OK. I handled it. Put your hand in my pocket, not the breast pocket.'

She felt his fingers, gentle against her. He slid the wad out of her pocket and stared at the russet coloured banknotes.

'For the Centre,' she said, watching his face.

'For the Centre,' he said slowly. 'Thanks. That's... good.'

'I got more.' She pulled back the sheet from the top corner of the paintings. 'Art, like he said, worth real money.'

Paul stared at the swirling yellow and red and green

of the Ackermann. He reached out and touched it. 'That's brilliant. You done good. I waited for you. How did you get them?'

'It sort of happened. He owed me.'

'Oh.' He was silent, his gaze inward. He looked back at the money. 'Enough to get the Centre going. Proper legal advice. Take on the landlords, take on the council.'

She kept her eyes on his. Deep within them she could see tiny images of her face reflected back at her.

'So what happened? Up there.'

'I think he slipped me something, I was completely out of it. He got me up there. I couldn't stop him. He's got a cupboard full of pills in his flat.'

He halted and stood there gripping her arm, his eyes sharp as knives. 'The bastard! I'll…'

'It's OK. I handled it. It's not your problem.' She looked down at his hand. 'You're hurting me.'

'I'm sorry. I'd like it to be my problem. Please.'

They walked on slowly, so close their shoulders were touching. Ade continued: 'Listen, it's like this. He bought me a drink, he paid some money, so he thinks he owns me. Could have been anyone but it was me, my body, he used me. So I did something. I got even.'

'You didn't do anything stupid, did you? After he…? Not like Webster?'

'It was the booze and maybe pills. Like I said, I handled it. You don't get even, not really. You do the best you can.'

After a while she felt his fingers squeeze hers. 'I'm not really a vampire,' she said. 'Or a super-hero. Or a revenge artist.'

She could feel the sun warm on her face. Somewhere

above them was the faint song of the blackbird. You had to be up early to hear the birds in the city.

'He had paintings,' she said, 'all sorts of paintings. And some sculptures. He deals in them, it's all a tax-dodge. And he's a bit of an amateur. He wants to be an artist. So I found some red paint.'

His dark eyes were like pools of oil, intent on her.

'I took a tiny dab of paint, on my little finger,' she said, 'and I marked the pictures and the drawings and the sculptures and the engravings. I marked them with two little marks, like wounds, just the kind of wounds teeth would make. Next to each other, on the throat, just here.'

She brushed her fingers ever so lightly against his neck.

'I marked all of them,' she said. 'There were quite a few. Then I found a knife, a small knife with a riveted wooden handle and a serrated blade and a sharp point, and I dipped the point in the red paint, thick as syrup, and I twisted it round. I went into the bedroom, and I bent down over him as he lay there asleep. And I took the knife and I touched it very gently against his throat, twice, close together, just where I could see the artery pulsing, where he'd been dribbling in his sleep out of the corner of his mouth. I made two red marks, little marks, like very sharp teeth would make.'

She held him very tight against her and pressed her mouth against his throat, very gently, oh so gently, and she bit, not hard, just enough, and she felt his body jerk against her. She stroked him, running her hand from the hair-line right down his cheek and slid her mouth into the little whorl of baby-hair, just by his ear, and whispered:

'And I took the knife and I dipped it in the paint again and I let the paint trickle all along the blade, and I wiped the handle and I laid it there, on the pillow, just where he'd see it first thing when he woke up and the first thing he'd smell would be the paint, red as blood. And I wiped my fingers on the sheet, very carefully, and I left him, fast asleep.'

She stood there without moving, feeling Paul close to her, her arms round him. It was just them against the city, with the blackbird singing its heart out, greeting the day.

'I handled it Paul. I didn't lose control. He's a bastard. Just like all the other bastards in the city. We won. We're going to sort him out.'

She nursed the hatred within her, smouldering, under control. *That fat, needy man, who wants friends and loves art and doesn't pay tax and thinks he can use me just 'cos he wants to. Justice. It's not paying him back, it's not revenge, it's justice.*

He looked up at her. 'Can't I help?'

'You're helping. You never tried to use me. You sorted Vinny. You saved me that night, after Webster. You looked after me. You help me all the time.'

'You're a powerful woman. A man gotta be careful near you.'

'Come on. The café'll be open soon.'

18

'Big breakfast, double hash browns, black pudding.' Ade said. 'Twice.'

Paul grunted. He still had his hand in hers. 'Mine's the vegetarian.' He stared at the menu over the counter. 'You got porridge?'

'Sorry love. No call for it.'

'Weetabix?'

'Sorry, love. Veggie'll take a minute. Have to find it.'

'And a glass of milk, skimmed.'

'Sorry love. Full fat.'

Ade grinned at him and bit into her sausage. Warm fat spurted into her mouth.

'Lovely food,' she said, her mouth still full. 'Best café for miles.'

'How can you eat that? Cows are people too. Besides it's a week off your life every bite you take.'

'Yeah, I should worry about that. I love sausages.'

'Veggie burger, diet coke,' said the young woman with flax-blond hair and milky blue eyes, slapping them down in front of Paul. He handed her the coins.

'Thanks.' He glanced round the room. 'But how did you know it was me?'

'You're the only one ever eats 'em. We got 'em 'specially for you. She asked us.'

She pointed to Ade.

'That's nice.'

He put down a couple more coins.

'You should see what they look like before they're cooked.'

The young woman winked and was gone.

'She's got such pure skin,' he said.

'Yeah, it's the ten hour days, and the grease.'

'So what we going to do?'

'Those pictures are worth real money. Besides that's what they love, stuff that goes up in value, even in a recession. They're portable, you can show off with them, you can take them to the Cayman Islands in your private jet, no accounting. You want a favour? You hand one over. It's a present so there's no tax. Revenue got their eye on the art market, but there's never any proof.'

'So we're international art thieves now.'

'National, I guess. Listen: we can't sell 'em, we can't take 'em to a gallery.' She waved her fork. 'We can ransom them. He pays the tax, he can have 'em back. Ronnie Wells'll pay up. He loves art, he said so. Besides they're worth it.'

Paul stared at her. 'You need someone to look after you. It's a big risk.'

'We're doing it for Morwen. You never met her. And we're doing it for Denny. Get some tax in that office. 'Cos she was the only one who stood up for Morwen. You got milk on your lip.'

He dabbed at it and she thought of Jessica, on her knees, dabbing at the carpet. She thought of Webster, his hand sliding towards her breast, she thought of his face, smirking at her, smirking at all of them. She thought of him in the lift, the gross body jammed against her, trapping her, the odour of wine and tobacco and stale breath. She thought of Ronnie Wells pulling her into the taxi. Her voice hardened.

'These people think they can piss on the rest of us. They are going to pay their tax. I don't care if he loves art. He'll pay. That's justice.'

'Here's luck,' said Paul.

He downed the rest of the milk in one.

Eleven a.m. the next day. Paul was waiting at the corner, looking the other way, his jacket wrapped tight round him, hands in pockets, his shoulders hunched up, though there was no wind and the winter sun felt warm on the skin. *He seems so frail,* she thought, *he needs a proper coat.* She let her feet click on the pavement. He whipped round, the smile lit up his face and her spirit soared. He had his arms round her.

'Missed you,' he whispered, his lips against her ear.

'It was only a day. I been busy.'

Yeah, she thought, *mainly in bed, sleeping, eating, watching TV, sending out for pizza, resting, sleeping. She'd needed the sleep. But she'd sorted things too.*

'Long time.'

They kissed and time slowed. The people walking past them seemed a hundred miles away.

'All clear?'

'I been checking. I kept moving around like you said. Some City of London cops went in but they didn't see me.

They been gone twenty minutes. There's only one person in there. Young bloke.'

'That's good.'

His face shone. They moved along the pavement, arms round each other, like any young couple out on the street on a Saturday in this fashionable area of the city. The galleries weren't really open yet, they didn't do much business until after lunch. It was a beautiful day, unseasonably warm.

Paul nodded towards the entrance. 'That's it. That's where we were last night.'

Ade slipped something out of her pocket.

'What you got?'

'Mobile – new, supermarket, five pounds. One call and it's in the river.'

'Cool. Five pounds for a call? They saw you coming.'

'Actually it was on special. Ninety-nine pee. Use it once and chuck it, straight away, they can't trace it to you.'

'Oh. You been watching movies?'

'It's on YouTube.'

They were passing a tall Georgian building with a heavily pilastered façade, just opposite the gallery. "Wells Fine Art". It looked different from the way it had last night with the light spilling out the door and the group of men on the pavement. In the light of day it seemed smaller but more imposing. She slowed and pulled Paul back into the shadow of one of the columns. No-one paid any attention to them. She could see the gallery's reception desk through the window across the street. She clasped Paul close to her and clicked Speedcall 1 on the phone.

'What's happening?'

'Nothing. There's a bloke there, he's picking up the phone.'

Ade heard a clipped nasal voice in her ear: 'Yes?'

She glanced up. It was Grant, the sharp-faced young man of the half-finished drawing, in a sandy-coloured three-piece suit, not the same as the one last night.

'Can I speak to Ronnie Wells?'

'I'm afraid Mr' – he stressed the "Mr" – 'Wells will not be at the gallery today.'

'Can you take a message?'

'Afraid not. I suggest you call next week.'

'Too late then. I can only leave a message.' Ade was enjoying this.

'Please call later.'

Grant was ready to put the phone down.

'You don't like him, do you?'

'Pardon?' She saw him stiffen, like a hunting dog that's spotted a hawk.

'It's a message he definitely won't want to hear. About Tintoretto. And Ackermann.'

'Yes?'

Grant was bending his left arm awkwardly to reach into his jacket pocket.

'He wants to see the paintings again, look on Tower Beach before the next high tide. And pay your tax. All of it. Now.'

'I'm sorry?'

Grant had dragged a mobile out of his pocket and was trying to dial with his thumb while still holding the landline receiver. *The same digit three times. Why's that so difficult?*

'He'll know what we mean. He's got two hours.'

Ade pressed End Call.

'We'll go for a stroll.'

As soon as they'd turned the corner, she dropped the phone and stamped on it. Paul scooped up the pieces. They scattered them off London Bridge.

'So what's he going to find on Tower Beach?'

Ade looked down at the river. A tug for the Battersea Project was making its way towards them, the string of barges behind it heavy in the water, the diesels throbbing, the fumes ascending more or less vertically in the still air. Further down she could see the sunlight glinting on the turrets of Tower Bridge. Webster, Ronnie Wells, CI Mayland, she felt equal to any of them.

'He'll find a photocopy of the paintings with the trademark red spots on the throat. And a note: 'You owe the Revenue, you've had the assessment. You want your paintings back, pay up.' All nicely wrapped up in one of his bedsheets. And, of course, the cards.'

'Yeah. The cards make all the difference, maybe.'

She hugged him to her. 'He owes me. This is something I have to do.'

Paul nodded. He looked out over the river. 'I want to be part of it. Don't leave me out. I'd do anything for you.'

'You're part of this. But you have to trust me.'

He had both his arms round her.

'I'd trust you with my heart's blood.'

19

They strolled past City Hall in a cheerful mob of tourists. They walked hand-in-hand, very close to each other. After a while they paused to lean on the parapet over the Thames.

'People just love the sunshine in winter,' said Ade. 'Look! That's the third man in shorts so far. Doesn't suit him.'

Ade stared at the Tower of London opposite them. It had always seemed like a Toy Town castle to her, with its neatly-crenelated battlements and slim towers capped with slate candle-snuffers. The beach in front of it was mostly out of the water and crowded with people, families, tourists, office workers who'd escaped for an hour, all out there in the pale sunshine. A group of children in sunhats were playing with an inflatable yellow dragon. *They must be chilly*, she thought. *Hope someone's got an eye on them.*

The blue-grey waves of the river rolled past, trailing streamers of weed up-stream from the pillars of Tower Bridge. *Tide's turned.* She could smell the dankness that hung over the water.

'No sign of him,' said Paul. 'Christ, it's the cops!'

He pulled at her arm. Ade caught a siren in the distance growing louder.

'Take it easy,' she said. 'We're just tourists, watching the show.'

A police car roared onto Tower Bridge, its light flashing, and halted, slewed across the carriageway at the far end. Two motor-bikes appeared, moving slowly through the crowd on the embankment opposite them and stopped. The cops dismounted and started to order people back onto the bridge. A group of policemen spilled onto the beach at the quay end and ran along it, shouting at the holiday-makers to get out of their way. People were crowding onto the steps. Someone shouted out and the inflatable dragon bobbed, swung round and plunged away from the beach, a small boy clinging to it with his arms round its neck, laughing.

One of the cops waded out, grabbing for the rope, just missing it. People were shouting. Ade saw a young man in running shorts balance gracefully on the rail of the bridge and pivot forward, arms outstretched, head neatly tucked in. He entered the water without a splash and started after the inflatable, front crawl. By now the cop had got his boots off and threw himself clumsily into the water after him. People were packing the edge of the bridge. She could hear cheering like they thought it was a race.

Paul touched her arm. 'Check the armbands. City of London.'

Ade nodded towards the end of the beach. She was in control. 'Right on cue. And doing just as they've been told.'

The motorcycle cops were rummaging in the flotsam piled against the jetty by the tide. One of them straightened holding up a square white object. The other touched him on the shoulder and pointed at the water lapping round their feet. They moved smartly away, up the steps, onto their bikes and were gone.

Ade and Paul walked slowly back through the crowd along the embankment hand in hand. It was a splendid day. They'd soon be on the Thames path, leading up to the Tate Modern and the Globe Theatre.

'You. Hold it there!'

A policewoman stepped out, barring their way. Ade felt her heart jerk in her breast. A line of police marched out in front of them, facing outwards at the crowd, clearing the area leading up to the main entrance to City Hall. People were pressing forward all round them. A motorcycle engine roared and a police bike mounted the kerb followed by a sleek black Daimler with a crest on it which halted at an angle to the road.

'Relax,' whispered Paul, squeezing her hand. 'It's democracy in action.'

The chauffer pulled open the car's door and a plump older man with small eyes, wearing a rumpled suit and an obvious wig, got out. He paused, surveying the crowd, as if weighing up whether to wave and press hands or ignore them. Ade felt his eyes directly on her. He sniffed, turned and lumbered towards the entrance. A young woman, meticulously made up, in a tight business suit, high heels and blond hair pinned back, got out on the other side of the car and walked after him, carrying an armful of files. She muttered something and he turned, smiling warmly, and waved to the crowd. His shirt was hanging half out of his trousers.

'"Votes", not "voters", "votes" – that's what she said to him,' Paul muttered.

'White wine,' said Ade, 'Large one.'

The barman, who looked younger than her fourteen-year old nephew, capped a hand behind his ear.

'Wine,' she shouted.

He nodded and recited 'Sauvignon, Chardonnay, Shiraz, Pinot, Merlot, Burgundy, Champagne,' as if it was one word.

'Never mind,' she said. 'Draft Guinness.'

She sipped at the bitter cloying soothing liquid.

'Cheers! This stuff's as good as a health drink, you know.' Paul grinned and clinked his glass against hers, slopping beer onto the bar.

'Do you think it'll work?'

'Ronnie's got his instructions. He'll pay up.'

He jogged her arm. A news strapline ran across the bottom of the TV screen above the bar: 'Massive ex gratia tax payment. 'Civic Duty' says city fat cat.'

'Can you turn the sound up?' he said to the barman.

The bulky man wearing a torn leather jacket next to him muttered something.

'What?' said Paul. 'I'm trying to listen.'

'Bastards. Hate 'em.'

'Who? Business men? Fat Cats?'

'Business, tax, hate all of them.' He downed the rest of his drink in one.

Ade felt Paul's mouth against her ear. 'Did you get any of that?'

She wrapped her arm round him and held him against her. 'Yeah, I got enough. He's paid up. No-one said anything about the pictures. They're keeping quiet. And I've got another idea.'

'What?'

'Tell you outside.' The elation was surging through her. She'd won, they'd won! 'Too many people here. Drink up.'

'He's paid up!' said Ade, standing next to Paul in the pool of light from the pub door. 'He's paid up, he's paid up, he's paid up!'

She flung her arms round him. 'He didn't argue about the assessment, he just paid up. Like I said, he wanted the paintings back and he knew he owed the money, so he just paid.'

'You are so cool.' Paul squeezed her tight and kissed her, just under her ear.

'And he sent the receipt to the *Financial Times* like it said and it's on their website and the Revenue press-released it to encourage the others, and it all goes through Denny's office. With Webster and this one she's brought in so much cash they'll have to promote her. Might give her an OBE. There's nothing about the paintings 'cos they don't want anyone else doing it. City of London police. They look after the city.'

'We cracked it,' he sang, 'we've just cracked it.'

'Vampires and ransoms. Fear of the devil, fear of god. They paid up and we made 'em do it.'

'Should be drinking champagne.'

'No, keep a low profile.'

'OK, Guinness.'

'No, champagne.'

They were on Bankside, leaning back on one of the benches, staring up at the sky over the river. The paving stones, damp after rain, glistened in the streetlights. He passed her the bottle.

'Careful, that's good stuff – the '89.'

'How would you know?'

He had an arm round her. 'Can we stay here for ever?' He pressed his face against her cheek.

'Just for a little while.' She thought how good it was, to have him nestling against her. 'We've got things to do.'

A halo hung round the streetlights in the misty air and, over it all, the moon was rising, casting a soft radiance over London.

'So where're the pictures?'

'Wrapped round my chest,' said Ade, 'under my tits. I took them out of the frames.' She giggled and swigged the last of the wine. 'They've been there since this morning. A bit sweaty, but it's oil paint.'

'Wow,' said Paul, 'you are number one: that's twice.'

She dipped her head in acknowledgement. He's right, she thought.

'Now we've got to give the paintings back.'

'Why? They've worth money.'

'No. Too risky to hang onto them. Besides they have to know we're serious: pay your tax, you get your paintings back. That's the deal.'

'So what do we do? Left-luggage locker, dump them on an all-night bus, post them?'

'No, here's the plan: we'll leave them somewhere where no-one'll look for them and where they're bound to be found.'

20

They kept on up the path, dodging through the crowds of tourists and workers making their way east. She led Paul into the shadow under London Bridge.

'Where are we going now?' he asked.

She kissed him. 'Tate Modern. Look at pictures.'

She took his hand. Soon she was striding past the grove of newly planted silver birch in front of the gallery, her feet crunching on the gravel, the great rust-brown chimney towering above her.

This isn't Toy Town, she thought. *It looks like a real castle, and the Millennium Bridge is a silver drawbridge. You wouldn't want to make trouble with someone who lived in that. Just back down the road, that's where Webster's offices are.* She shivered and pulled her coat round her. *Bet he's in on the works of art scam. Think of those paintings he had in his office.*

'You OK?' said Paul.

'It's nothing. Have you ever been inside a real Art Gallery? The other night doesn't count.'

'No. What for?'

She loved this building. She remembered the first time Morwen had brought her here, how excited she'd been when they'd walked out on the gantry over the vast pit of the Turbine Hall, the glowing disc of the eye of the storm above them seeming to fill the whole space with radiance. *The Weather Project*, such an everyday title. She remembered how the light glinted from Morwen's eyes, as she craned her neck upwards, how she twisted her body to look on all sides, how she peered over the parapet. It seemed the right place to take the pictures.

She led Paul through the entrance into the glass-panelled atrium, the shop behind them and the cavern of the Turbine Hall to the side.

'Good, isn't it?' she said. 'Now, see that woman there, standing over by the desk?'

'The one with waist-length hair, smart jeans and the big sign? Looks like a lollypop lady only she ain't, not with those specs?'

'She's a guide waiting to take people round. The sign's got a picture on it. I want you to go up to her and point at that painting, the big one behind her, and tell her you've got a five-year-old who can do better than that.'

'I ain't got a five-year-old. I'd have told you.'

'I know, Paul, it's something people say. But just do it. And if she starts explaining, argue with her. Shout. Make a scene. Get everyone there.'

'But they'll throw me out.'

'That's the idea. You distract them while I dump the paintings. See you outside in ten minutes.'

When she came back, eight minutes later, pretty well all the museum staff were grouped round the exit staring out, all talking at once. The guide was looking dazed, her hair dishevelled, polishing her outsize glasses on a paisley scarf. The picture had come off the post, and another guide in a leather jacket was holding it out to her. A guard in a uniform that was too big for him stood next to her, stirring at tea in a large china mug. Floodlights had come on in the Turbine Hall. *Knew I could rely on Paul*, she thought.

A couple of guards came in, swaggering. The group seemed to shrink away from them. Ade moved nearer, pretending her attention was caught by a modernist poster of a giant silver airship.

The one with the square face and the crew-cut slapped some dust off his hand: 'Little runt. You won't see him again.'

'I'm sure he had a point of view, it was just, well, he insisted, and then he wanted to take over and be the guide himself,' said the woman with the glasses. 'You didn't hurt him, did you?'

'Oh, he'll be all right miss. Just showed him off the premises.'

'We insisted,' said the smaller guard. Ade noticed he had a scar on the point of his chin. They laughed.

Ade realised they were G4S, not gallery staff. She pushed past them. No sign of Paul. She felt her heart contract. Outside it was evening. There was a bank of fluffy grey clouds lit up from within by a pink glow over the Thames. A small figure was squatting, half-lying, hunched down at the edge of the shadows at the far end of the façade. She waved and he tried to get up and fell back. She ran towards him.

'Paul! Are you OK?'

He smiled at her. 'I'm fine.' There was a fleck of blood at the corner of his mouth. 'Did good, didn't I?'

'Oh Paul. You did wonderful.' She was kissing him hard, holding him to her.

'Careful,' he mumbled. 'Not too tight.'

Then he was kissing her back, eyes closed, in the rosy light of evening, the river flowing past them, through the city, out to the sea, the light gleaming from a million windows, towers, flats, houses, churches, and a sharp clean smell in the air.

21

The taxi whirled through the dark streets, towards the east. Ade held Paul against her, her jacket round him, warming his body against hers.

'I never meant this to happen. I'm so sorry.' She stroked her hand gently down his cheek. His skin felt so cold.

'It's OK. I wanted to help. I want to help you all I can.'

He broke off to cough and she felt him wince. She had to explain. Should have told him the whole thing before, but there hadn't been time, there was never time.

'It was meant to be a diversion. I slipped the pictures into one of those big racks in the shop while no-one was looking. It just seemed the right place. And I left some cards'

'It would have been all right. Those guards just wanted to shove me out the door. But a couple of City of London cops in their red and white armbands came along and that's when it started. It's OK, I been on demos, I got curled up.'

'But I never thought they'd hit you. I should have explained everything first. I'm so sorry.'

He took her hand. 'Not a problem.' He smiled. 'You needed me for that, didn't you?'

'I couldn't have done any of it without you.'

'You're smart.' He held her hand tight in his. 'But you got to be careful.'

He paused.

'There were some students there on the bridge and they started filming on their mobile phones and that stopped it. One of the students was really worried about me; she was typing everything into her phone. She said I ought to go to A and E, I should file a complaint, they'd be witnesses. I said it was OK, I didn't want a fuss, but really I wanted to be alone.'

He looked up at her and she stroked a lock of hair off his face.

'Because I knew you'd come.'

Nadia was there at the squat and Johnno. They helped her bring Paul in, Johnno making odd little noises of sympathy. Casey said something about how he knew she'd bring trouble, and Johnno just pushed him back through the door into the passageway and held it shut. Ade looked at Nadia and she nodded and helped her bring him up the stairs. She brought warm water from the stove and clothes and a large pink towel and ushered Johnno away. Then he was on the bed and the light was streaming through the window and Ade was closing the door and he was sitting up, just looking at her.

'Lay back,' she said pushing very gently at his chest. 'Take it easy. First, I'm going to wash you.'

She unlaced his shoes, left and right, and slipped them off his feet. She reached up and carefully unbuckled his belt and folded back the strap. She undid the button at the top of his jeans and pulled at the zip. Then she crouched at the foot of the bed and tugged at the trouser legs. He reached down and eased them over his hips and she slipped them off. She folded them and placed them on the floor.

She slipped his arms out of his jacket. *His clothes are so thin,* she thought, *the material cheap and worn.* She unbuttoned the shirt and opened it and ran her hand across the smooth skin of his chest. She felt him tense under her, and relax. She folded the shirt and jacket and placed them on the jeans. Then she took up a cloth, tested the water with her elbow and soaked it, wringing it out. She sponged him with long slow strokes, his feet, his calves, his thighs, his chest, his arms, his neck, his hands, opening them out and rubbing gently at the palms and along his fingers. She took the towel in both hands and dried him down, patting his body, wrapping it round him. He was so thin she could feel the bones in his chest.

'Ade,' he said.

'Shhh.'

She took the warm wet cloth and washed his belly, his hips, his buttocks. She rubbed gently, very gently across his groin. She put down the cloth and dried him, patting him dry. His eyes were bright in the dark, fixed on her.

Then she stood up in the moonlight by the window and slipped off her own clothes, letting them fall in an untidy pile on the floor. She crossed to the bed and knelt beside him.

'Ade,' he said. 'I love you.'

'Shhh. I know.'

'Ade, maybe later. You've had such a terrible time.'

'Shhh. So have you. We won. This is what I want.'

'So do I. So much. Since we were first together, running over London Bridge.'

She laid a finger softly across his lips and straddled him and reached down and slid his penis into her, hard and smooth. He gasped and she pressed down on him. She leaned forward and rocked against him. She could feel him thrusting up into her with all the force in his slender body. She moved, holding herself hard against him, faster and faster. She could hear him making tender little noises, then he was crying out 'Ade!', 'Ade!' and he was surging into her and her body was crammed with such delight that she fell forward onto his breast and his arms were round her and he was whispering into her ear 'Ade!', 'Ade!', 'Ade!'

Much later they lay there in the dark, the moon sinking away behind the skyline, the stars high up above them.

'Paul,' she said, 'are you awake?'

'Yes.'

'I love you.'

She felt his arms tighten round her.

'Tax-woman,' he murmured. 'Robyn Hood. Super-hero.'

'With issues.'

'Everyone's got issues. We handled them.'

22

Ade woke once in the night, her head filled with dreams. The moon gleamed at the edge of a vast continent of cloud. Nothing else was visible. She'd been flying in her dream, swooping down over the city, the wind fresh on her face, the taste of the clouds on her tongue, the cape rippling out behind her. She mantled like a hawk, hovering for an instant over Trafalgar Square, then up, up, into a moonless sky, stars gleaming cold and ancient, infinitely far above her. Below she could see the city spread out, ribbons of light along the arterial roads, the housing estates dark, the roads speckled with streetlights. Below her all was safe, all was secure, and in her was the knowledge that it was all, all of it, because she was here, watching over all the people of London.

She raised herself on one elbow and felt the night air cool on her skin. Paul lay curled towards her, his hand under his cheek, sleeping, perhaps dreaming too. Tomorrow she would ask him. She pulled up the duvet round his shoulders and hers and sank back on the pillows.

Someone was hammering on the door of the squat, regular blows, thud, thud, thud. Ade was suddenly awake. Sunlight was streaming through the window. They'd overslept. She felt Paul stir against her.

The letter-box rattled at the front of the building, next to the shop-window.

'Open up! Police.'

'Stay there,' she whispered, slipping on her jeans and fleece and starting down the stairs. They were at the front entrance, the one no-one used because it was too public. She slammed back the bolts and wrenched open the door, flicking her hair out of her eyes. Sergeant Jones stood right in front of her, not a foot away, his gloved fist raised. She could see the white shape of a police car behind him.

'Ah,' he said. 'Ms Corey. Found you. We're good at finding people.' He half-turned and called over his shoulder. 'Got her.'

Ade pushed hard at the door, but he had his foot jammed against the threshold.

'Not so fast,' he said.

If she'd had her high heels on she could've stamped on his foot. Her heel would stab through boot-leather, no problem. He shouldered the door open.

'Mind if I come in? Thanks.'

'I haven't seen a warrant,' said Ade. 'Or identification come to that.'

'Don't be like that. We've been introduced. You can always come down the station. Nasty people down there. Not polite like us.'

He touched the peak of his cap and pushed past her down the gloomy corridor into the squat. Mayland stood in front of her.

'Good morning,' she said. 'Thank you for inviting us in.'

'I didn't, you're like bloody vampires,' muttered Ade. 'First rule, never ask 'em in.'

'Heard it before,' said Mayland, glancing down the hall. 'Anyone else here?'

She placed a hand on Ade's chest and pushed her against the wall.

'You should go to the gym more.'

Ade stared at her without saying anything. *Bastard*, she thought.

Jones appeared at the other end of the hall, the light from the stairs behind him. 'All clear back here. No one under the table.'

'Upstairs,' said Mayland.

'It's all right.' Ade gripped Mayland's wrist with both hands. She couldn't shift it. 'It's only Paul. He's sleeping.'

'Weight-lifting,' said Mayland. 'Keep some weights in the office. Makes a difference.'

Ade heard a door slam back against the wall upstairs, then Paul's voice and Jones shouting at him. She winced.

'We told you about Mr Affarn, when we came to see you in your office after the attack on Mr Webster. That led to a lot of trouble for everyone. Now we've got theft of valuable pictures from Mr Ronnie Wells. Extortion. It's going to make more trouble. He's a prominent city art-dealer. Very respectable, deals with the most distinguished clients in the City. And your Mr Affarn was seen yesterday, near where one of the pictures was found. Interviewed by two of my officers in fact. Is that news to you?'

'I don't know what you're talking about.' *Keep your voice level*, she thought. *Don't drop your eyes.*

'Ah,' said Mayland, in her pleasant, reasonable voice. 'Here's Mr Affarn.'

133

Ade glanced down the corridor. She saw Paul first, stumbling, then Jones behind him, shoving him forward.

'Nothing to do with her,' said Paul. 'Leave her out of it.'

'Out of what, sir?'

'Whatever you're on about. She's a tax-inspector. You should be on the same side – the tax pays your salary, doesn't it?'

Mayland took off her cap with her free hand. She released Ade and ran her other hand across her head. Ade reached out and grasped Paul's hand. She realised how small it was, she could fit it comfortably inside hers.

'Yes,' Mayland said. 'Sides. Our side is the City of London. We look after the City. We know you, Mr Affarn: public disorder, incitement to riot, Occupy, all that. Not a friend to the City are you? Now we've got these.'

She flipped a card out of her breast-pocket. Ade could see the tiny figure silhouetted against the full-moon. 'Occupy Man and Tax-woman. That's what led us to the pair of you.'

'So what?' said Ade. 'It's no crime to print a business card.'

Mayland replaced the card in her pocket.

'It's a criminal offence to steal valuable paintings. It's a criminal offence to assault people and terrorise them.'

'Has anyone complained? I read in the paper that Mr Webster said he wants people to forget the matter.'

'If only they would. Mr Webster and Mr Wells are not nice men. I told you to be careful about your associates. They prefer to keep things out of the papers. My duty is to the City of London. There's been all this rubbish about vampires in the City. Now there's stuff about massive tax payments.'

She glanced at Paul then fixed her eyes back at Ade.

'The City's like a great ocean liner. A shock's gone through it. Everyone's felt it, passengers and crew, first class and steerage. Could be driftwood. Could be an iceberg. We don't want everyone making for the life-boats do we? Maybe there aren't enough life-boats.' She leaned forward. 'Panic. That's not what we want. Not a good thing for the City.' She smiled, showing neat white teeth. 'Glad to say we're putting the lid on it. Back to business as usual.'

'So you've burst into this house and pulled innocent people out of bed to tell us you've got no case and everything's normal? I wish to make a complaint.'

'Complaints forms at the station. We're here to explain what will happen. You will drop all enquiries into Mr Webster and Mr Wells and all,' she stressed the word, 'their associates. And matters will rest. See? Business-friendly. I'm trying to help you. On your side.'

'No. I have a duty too. To the Revenue and the tax-payer. No taxes, no NHS. Maybe no police.' She squeezed Paul's hand.

'In that case we will need to pursue enquiries further. Against Mr Affarn. We believe he may be involved in printing these neat little cards. That would be conspiracy. Funny. Sometimes you get a longer sentence for conspiring to do something than for actually doing it.'

The Chief Inspector looked up at Ade, her eyes like pebbles. Ade realised that she had no idea what Mayland was thinking. 'Mr Affarn will come with us.'

Mayland nodded. Jones forced Paul's other arm up against his back and pushed him forward, wrenching his hand away from Ade's. Paul's eyes were wide with fear. She felt her throat constrict. He twisted his head round: 'It's OK, see you later. At the café.'

'No, wait. He lives here, you have no right. Let him go. I'll slow things down.' She had her hand on Paul's arm. Mayland knocked it away.

'No,' she said. 'Paul will come with us for now.' Her dark eyes were still staring directly into Ade's. 'For clarity.'

Paul twisted his head round as Jones forced him down the steps. 'I'll be OK. Don't listen to her, you can't trust them,' he shouted. Jones put his free hand on top of Paul's head and pushed him down and through the rear passenger door of the police car.

'I think that's everything,' said Mayland, with her usual smile. 'You had your chance. Don't forget your promise. Thank you for your assistance.'

She walked smartly to the car and got in.

'Check your shadows,' shouted Ade after her.

'Heard it before.'

Ade slammed the door shut, bolted it and moved away, back to the kitchen. The sun was shining down into the garden. Ten minutes she thought. Ten minutes and everything's different. They've got Paul. I have to get him back.

Something moved in the garden and she started back from the window. There was a scraping noise at the door. She didn't know if it was locked. She ran her hand down to find where the bolt was, then she heard Johnno's voice: 'Have they gone now?'

She pushed the door open. Johnno stared at her. He had the hood of his sweat-shirt up, so she couldn't really see his face. She put her hand on his shoulder. She could feel him trembling.

'Johnno. It was the cops. They took Paul. But we're going to sort it out.'

Somewhere glass shattered. Johnno made a whimpering noise, grabbed her arm and pointed. Nadia was standing very upright, by the greenhouse, her arm outstretched, her fist punched through one of the windows. She slowly withdrew her arm and rested her fingers on the edge of the broken glass.

'Nadia!' Ade shouted. As she watched, Nadia broke off a triangle of glass and held it, examining it, the sun flashing on it as she turned it in her hand. She seemed intent on the point of the triangle. Ade jerked free of Johnno and started towards her. Nadia spread out the fingers of her free hand and drew the point slowly across her palm. She stood there, motionless, staring at the blood as it dripped from the heel of her hand onto the grass.

'Nadia,' Ade said, not loudly.

Nadia dropped the shard. Ade heard it shatter on the path. She held her hand out to Ade. The skin was pink, the blood almost black against it.

'It comforts you,' she said, her face calm. 'You can control the pain.'

Ade took Nadia by the wrist and led her slowly back towards the house. The light was so bright it hurt her eyes.

'It's OK,' she said. 'We'll get Paul back. Let's find something to put on your hand.'

23

Ade sat on the train, leaning against the window and staring out, the rhythm of the wheels drumming away beneath her. She tried to find words for it, but they wouldn't fit and they became jumbled. She felt empty. She saw Paul's face in the darkness, the expression in his eyes as Jones forced him down into the car. *I can't ever go back to the squat*, she thought. *Casey was right. I just brought them trouble.*

She looked round at the other commuters. A young man sat opposite her, his head in a cycling magazine. He looked up at her and she turned her head. The older woman next to her, smart suit, hand-stitched brief-case on her lap, was reading the *Financial Times*. 'Christmas Comes Early for the Revenue' read the headline. She stared at the paper:

"'Recent events have led to an unprecedented inflow of tax from the UK financial sector. "This underlines the success of our relaxed approach to tax collection", said Chancellor Spalden today, announcing further cuts in Revenue staff. "We trust the City and the City trusts us. Why waste money on tax gatherers?"

"Britain's revenue service is the finest in the world," responded Dr Fingle for the Opposition. "The Chancellor should not try to divert attention from multiple failures by attacking hard-working public servants. He has done nothing to address the unease following the City Vampire scare and failed to halt the wave of copycat muggings."'

I have to get Paul out, but... Her thoughts spiralled away. *They need Paul in the squat, they're his family.* Then Morwen was there in her mind too, and it was Morwen that first day coming towards her in the office, not Morwen behind the glass screen in Bronzefield.

They were running scared, those bastards in the city. For some reason. Maybe word about the Model had got out, and they'd all seen Webster pay up. They knew he wouldn't meet an assessment unless he had to, so they'd guessed that the revenue knew a lot more than it ever had about whose snout was in which trough. No-one wanted to be last, you might end up in court with the people you did business with turned Crown's evidence. Cool. That's what Paul would say. Then there were the muggings.

If she stopped the investigation into Webster, Paul would be OK, they'd let him out, she'd see Paul again, but then Webster and Ronnie Wells and all of them had won, and she had lost and Morwen had lost and it had all been for nothing.

If she kept on, the money would come in and maybe they wouldn't cut social housing and the health service and child care and the buses and the railways and the carers for old people and the fire service and everything else quite so much.

She'd see him again, she heard it drumming out from the wheels. She'd see him again. *Not like that, I'm not letting them beat me.*

She stood up and pushed past the businesswoman and off the train. She walked up the escalator, past a huge bespangled Christmas Tree and a man dressed as a teddy bear shaking a tin for the Food Bank and handing out wine gums, and out onto the street. No-one had even started thinking about the Christmas decorations in the office yet and Christmas was nearly there.

She had to find a way through all this, she had to make it all work. Why were there so many people on the pavement, so many people in her way? The vampire scare was over, that was obvious. A portly man in a dove-grey overcoat lumbered in front of her. She dodged round him. The young woman in the red anorak was nowhere to be seen. A stooping man with a scrawny dog on a piece of string thrust a sign at her: "Ex-Army, no job, no home, no dole."

She hurried past, then stopped, went back and dropped all the change in her pocket into his hand.

'Thank you,' he shouted after her. 'God Bless.'

Ade stood in the doorway to Denny's office. The Special Advisor was in Denny's chair behind the desk, her hair tied tighter this morning and the make-up too carefully applied over her cheek-bones. Denny was on the upright chair between the bookcase and the window. She seemed somehow smaller than when Ade last saw her, folded in on herself. She looked up and gave Ade a warm smile.

The advisor fixed her eyes on Ade. 'Close the door. Sit.'

'Good morning,' said Ade. The advisor did not respond.

'My Minister is concerned,' she said after a moment. 'Seriously concerned.'

She touched the tips of her fingers together.

'First we have a violent assault on one of your cases. Not good. We have the police interviewing Revenue staff, most notably yourself, in this office. Not good. Then we have all these rumours about vampires in the city. Not good. Then we have an upward trend in receipts, led by this office. Good. You've seen the FT, of course. Then there's a massive ex gratia payment, again through this office. Good news for you, record income. Then there's a rumour about ransom demands and police involvement. Unconfirmed. Not good. Not business-friendly. Not at all.'

She paused and frowned at Denny.

'Then there have been questions in parliament about extortionate Revenue tactics. Not good.' She sighed. 'Then her Majesty's loyal opposition starts talking about bloodsucking fat cats and muggings in the city, not good. The tabloids love it. Not good.'

She leaned forward.

'Ms Corey. I make that seven "Not goods" and two "Goods". You're five down. Have you anything to say?'

'I know no more than anyone else about events in the City. But they do seem to be helping the Revenue in its mission of tax collecting. Naturally I'm delighted to work as part of an excellent team in an effective office.'

Denny nodded.

'Yes,' said the blond woman. Ade could see the grey at the roots of her hair. 'The politics of tax collecting is not simple. I recall I encouraged you to be more business-friendly in your methods. In particular, in relation to Mr Webster. Business-friendly. Being stabbed in the neck is not business-friendly.'

'Are you accusing me?' Ade felt a tightness in her chest. 'I can't believe….'

'No one is making any accusations whatsoever, Ms Corey. But let's not waste time. We think it appropriate…' she smiled over the word, '…for you and the Revenue to part company. Thank you for your service.'

The advisor bowed her head slightly. Ade stared at her. *She wants me to say something, to protest. Tough.*

'Clear your desk. One month's pay in lieu of notice. Taxed. Good day.'

She slid back her chair. Ade sat there, not moving.

Denny slammed her hand down on the desk. 'No!' She pushed herself to her feet. She was shaking her head from side to side. 'No. You can't do that. I will not allow it. My staff have rights. I simply won't allow it.'

'Calm yourself. Please sit down. Rights. I think we can dispense with those in this matter. I'm afraid there is a discrepancy in your expenses, a trip to …' she glanced at a slip of paper she held in the palm of her hand, 'Middlesbrough, has come to light. No evidence it was ever authorised. No one can find the paperwork, it's all disappeared. Been lost somewhere, you know how these things happen.'

She looked up, and Ade realised with a shock that the Advisor hated her. 'Puts you in a difficult position. One month's notice is generous.'

'But…' Ade said, 'that was three years ago, when I was training. I was shadowing Morwen.'

'Morwen Archer. That hardly helps your case, does it?' The advisor smiled. 'The decision was made upline.' She nodded towards the ceiling as if the Minister were floating somewhere above them.

Denny was talking over her, her voice unnaturally deep, the first time Ade had heard her raise it. 'She goes, I go. And half the office. Then you'll have some headlines. Close down the office that's brought all the money in from the fat cats. That means everyone out there on the street has to pay more. Not good.'

Denny plumped down into her seat and sat there breathing heavily.

Ade felt like everything was being taken away from her. The investigation's closed down, at least they'll let Paul out, they have to let Paul out.

'Don't think I'll stop,' she said. 'There's the union, there's appeals, there's the courts, there's newspapers, everything will come out, all the tax scams, how you tried to gag me.'

The advisor pursed her lips. She glanced from Denny to Ade. Neither of them spoke. She shrugged. 'Have it your way.' She paused for a moment, as if considering options, then said: 'I believe Mr Affarn is a friend of yours? He faces serious charges.'

Ade found herself gripping the edges of her chair so tight her fingers hurt. 'What's Paul, Mr Affarn, got to do with this?'

The advisor's eyes were fixed on her. She stretched out her right hand in front of her, palm upwards: 'Your resignation.' She stretched out her left hand, next to it: 'Mr Affarn's release.' She clapped her hands together: 'Deal?'

Ade felt her thoughts tumbling over one another. There was nothing she could hold on to. *We need the tax to get the housing and the health service and everything. I need Paul, to see him again. They need him in the squat.*

Somewhere right at the centre was Paul's face as Sergeant Jones forced him down into the car.

'And the squat? They leave those people alone?'

The advisor sniffed: 'Detail.'

Ade stared directly at her for a few moments. She felt as if her heart was breaking. Then she picked up a sheet of paper from Denny's desk, scribbled on it, folded it and flung it at the advisor.

'Deal,' she said.

The advisor opened the sheet, scanned it, cast one look at Ade, and stalked out of the room on her kitten heels.

24

Ade sat against the window at the back of the café, her coat wrapped round her. She stared at the Christmas tree on the counter, so heavy with baubles it seemed certain to over-balance. The street was dark, busy with people making for home. She listened to the conversations, everyone talking about what they'd have for Christmas dinner and how many they'd cook for. *Pigs in blankets,* she thought, *and white sauce, every time. And brandy butter. And brandy on the pudding. And sherry and red wine and white wine and the rest of the brandy.* She traced a trail across the condensation on the glass. *In her flat just up the road. With Paul. And Johnno and Nadia and all of them. Forget about everything else, just live your own life. No one could blame you, could they? Just for doing what everyone else did?*

'I knew you'd be here.'

Paul! Next second he had his arms round her and she luxuriated in the rich scent of his hair. Then he was kissing her.

'It's wonderful to see you,' she said. 'It's so good.'

She kissed him again. He was here, she'd made it happen, and it was the right thing to do. Denny would have done it, anyone would have done it. And she'd be with him, she'd help him, they'd do the best they could for homeless people.

'Ade, you got me out. I know it was you. How did you do it?'

'It's all right.' She cupped his face between her hands. 'It's all right.'

'You didn't... give up, did you? Let them all go? Like that copper said. He was sniggering, but I didn't believe him.'

'No, not that. It wasn't that.'

'Knew you wouldn't. I'd feel bad.'

'No, I packed in my job. I stepped out of it all. I just had to get you out.'

'You done that for me?' His eyes glistened. 'No-one's done anything like that for me before.'

'No problem. Everything's sorted.' She put a grin on her face. 'Just like you'd say, it's cool.'

Why do I feel my heart is breaking?

He took her hands and held them in his. 'But what will you do now?'

'Whatever comes next. I don't care. I used to care about all sorts of things, making people pay the right tax, getting on at work, my dad, all that, but I don't anymore.'

'But you're going to keep on aren't you? After Webster and the bastards?'

'Webster...' She looked at the window. 'That was part of my old life. Maybe you can't do everything.'

'Look, I'm happy, I'm with you, I'm so happy.' He was on his feet, his arms spread wide, shouting round to the café: 'Listen: I'm so happy!'

Silence. Ade looked round at all the pale faces staring

up at him. Then someone crashed a pan onto the stove in the kitchen. She sank down on the table, her hands in front of her face.

'Happy Christmas!' shouted someone.

'Merry Christmas', then 'Have a good one,' and the babble all round them redoubled.

'I'll never come here again,' she said.

'They've forgotten already.' He laid his hands on hers and leaned across the table, not smiling, his eyes fixed on hers. 'And it's true.'

He was holding her hands tight in his:

'So we're going to fix him, aren't we, this Webster? Come on. Tax-woman and Robyn, remember? Black buddy? How we going to do it?'

'I don't know. Every time I think about it, it seems harder. They all stick together, they're all up there and they've got so much. I got you out, that's something, isn't it? Every time we go after them, we get somewhere and they brush it aside. And it costs us, it costs the heart out of my breast. I thought maybe I wouldn't see you again, ever. Like Morwen, only worse.'

She felt the tears come, spilling over her cheeks. She didn't want him to see her crying like this.

'Don't cry. They ain't ever going to take me away from you. And you've got to keep fighting. I need you to do that.' He was wiping at her cheeks with the tips of his fingers, so softly, so gently.

'But I said I'd call off the investigation, go soft on them – business-friendly, they call it – so they'd let you out. Then I found I couldn't do that so I resigned. Chucked it all in. I did it for you.'

'Who cares? Forget the spreadsheets. We'll do a break-in, get all the evidence. He's a bastard. We could kidnap him.'

'It's not so easy. The evidence is all hidden somewhere in his computer. Kidnap's a serious offence. They'll lock you up forever.'

'The computer? No problem. I know kids can turn computers inside out and put 'em back together so you won't know.'

'It's not like that. This is the real world. It's secret, there are passwords, surveillance software. These people have got money, they've got the best security in the world. They've got the Minister, the City cops on their side. We've got to think about it.'

'Yeah, but it's who you are. They can sack you but they can't stop you being who you are.'

Ade glanced at the window. When the glass wasn't fogged up you could see the tops of the Canary Wharf skyscrapers towering above streets where people had once lived. Canada Square and, beyond that, the Shard and the Gherkin and Leadenhall and Fenchurch Street and Gresham Street and the Lloyd's Building and all the city spread out, the Thames snaking through it, everything linked up, everything tied together, the city exposed in Morwen's spreadsheets, Webster's city, the city she hated, the city she'd looked down into and through in her dream. The city of traders and brokers and dealers and tax-dodgers, everyone busy, hand over fist, all of them men, all of them joking, sneering, sniggering, all of them suddenly looking up, all of them pointing, all of them laughing at her. And beyond the Towers and the river, the streets and the buildings reaching further than she could see into, a blue distance of parks and bus-routes and schools and playgrounds and health centres and the flats and houses where everyone lived; all the people who really made up the city, who needed hospitals and pensions and ambulances and schools and clean water and nurseries and buses and colleges and a living wage, who needed a decent chance, who needed Morwen, who needed Morwen and Ade, who needed her.

'You all right?'

Ade had her face pressed hard against the glass. Paul was leaning over her, his arm round her, supporting her.

The table attendant stood next to him: 'Anything I can do? You want the full English? Real or veggie?'

'Real,' she said. 'He'll have unreal. And coke. Diet for him. And I want a Golden Syrup cookie.'

'OK.'

She winked, whipped round and picked her way expertly between the tables towards the serving hatch. No one paid her any attention. *She does that a thousand times a day,* thought Ade, *ten thousand times, and no-one ever notices her.* She thought about the Golden Syrup, the way it coated your tongue, the taste so powerful you couldn't think about anything else at all. *Is that my life? Nadia cut her hand because that was pain she could control. And I'm happy, I've got Paul back, we are going to live a normal life, just like anyone else. But there's something we need to sort first.*

'I've got an idea,' she said. 'Eat up, we're going to see someone. And does your phone do video?'

'What?'

She sat down again.

'I'll explain. We need someone who can get into Webster's office without anyone noticing, who does it every day, but first we need an address. Here's what we'll do.'

25

Ade led the way through the lobby and up the flight of marble stairs, her hand on the brass rail.

'Taste,' said Paul looking round. 'There's a lot of taste round here.'

'Just follow me. I'll do the talking. Bet you didn't know this place existed just off Bishopsgate, up the road from my office.'

They followed the staircase as it swept round a series of curves and came out at one end of a long gallery, lit by tall windows in one wall. Ade's immediate impression was of drapery, long velvet curtains, elaborately looped, even the cloths on the tables drooping down in exaggerated folds to the floor. The room seemed to absorb sound and almost absorb light. The thick dark carpet matched the curtains, and matched the polished black wood-block flooring showing round the edges. She heard Paul mutter 'taste' just behind her.

A thin grey man bent over towards her. He had a long lined face and a sharp nose. His evening dress seemed to hang in folds, like the curtains.

'May I help you, madam?' he asked in a slow grey voice.

'I would like to talk with Ms Samson.'

'Ms Samson. Whom shall I say?'

'Ade, and a guest. She'll know.'

'Ade.' He considered. 'Very well.'

A bell tinkled and a very young boy in a page's uniform, with brightly polished buttons and a centre parting, appeared at Ade's elbow. She could hear the tall man whispering to him. The page led the way down the gallery between tables where grey-haired men in suits of vintage style conversed in undertones. They seemed to draw back into the shadows when Ade glanced at them. The page stopped and inclined his head towards the next alcove, his lips compressed, bending forward slightly in imitation of the door-keeper.

'Denny!' said Ade. 'No one in the office knew where you were.'

Denny sat alone at a small table staring at the window. In front of her stood a half-bottle of sherry and a small tulip-shaped glass. She looked up at them without expression.

'You don't know how good it is to see you,' she said, warily, like a small boy unwrapping the birthday present from the aunt who always mixes him up with his big sister.

'I need your help. But why…?'

'I'm taking the afternoon off,' said Denny. 'First time in my career. Why not? It'll soon be Christmas.'

The pageboy slid a copy of the *Financial Times* onto the table. Denny glanced at him. 'Supposed to give him something,' she hissed.

Ade felt in her pocket, but Paul was already dropping some change into the boy's hand. He scrutinised it, frowned and marched off.

'Why don't you sit down?' said Denny. 'More the merrier. Have a drink.'

'No thanks. What's going on?'

'That damn special advisor's been again. Checking up. Everything business-friendly. Had to get the taste out of my mouth.'

'What is this place?' asked Paul. 'It's like the knees-up at the undertakers' social club.'

Denny laughed, a subdued creaking chuckle. 'Have you ever wondered why the City is in one place?'

'Sorry?'

'The City. Exists for financial transactions, insurance, trading, brokering, stocks and shares, loans, interest, deals. You can do all that on the web. Do it from your Blackberry, from your beach retreat on your Caribbean Island. So why do they all come and work here in the City? It's smelly, the property's expensive, the air's bad, the public transport is awful and you can't get a decent cup of coffee.'

'You lost me,' said Paul, smiling. 'Never struck me.'

'Word of mouth, old boy, that's why, word of mouth.' Denny leaned forward. 'Do deals with no emails, no evidence, no paperchain, no details that a nosey little fraud investigator or an inquisitive little tax inspector can dig up one day, so they come back to bite you. My word is my bond. Everyone thinks it's the seal of probity. Actually, it's the city's dirtiest secret. And why are they doing things they don't want anyone else to know about? Especially Ade and me?'

'Long speech for you, Denny. But you're right,' said Ade. 'And this is one of the places they come for word of mouth. Never knew how you got to be a member, though.'

'Don't ask. I just sit here and sip my tea. Except it's not tea today. No-one talks to me much, but I can watch what's going on, who's talking to whom, who isn't. You'd never believe…'

'I'd believe, Denny. But I came to ask you a favour. Just one. I need an address. It'll be in the database. She's a tax-payer and I've got the employer. Can you do that for me?'

Ade took the metal biro out of her pocket and tore the corner off the newspaper. She scribbled something and slid the piece of paper across the table. Denny glanced at it and nodded. She tore the paper in half, in quarters, then into tiny scraps.

'So you're still in business. You've made my day. Of course I can do this. Breach of the Official Secrets Act, but who cares?' She pulled herself to her feet. 'You go first and keep your head down. I'll be in touch.'

'Thanks, Denny. Come on, Paul.'

Ade led the way to the stairs. The thin grey man swivelled round in his place by the door, watching them go.

Ade kept her eyes on the office entrance, just across Gracechurch Street. She and Paul were sitting in the window of the coffee-shop in the mid-afternoon lull. The man behind the counter had grinned at her when they came in and put a couple of pains aux raisin on a plate and slid it across to them.

'On the house. Just don't tell the boss.'

Crowds of people wrapped up against the cold were sweeping past in both directions.

Ade checked her watch. 'Not long now.'

Paul sipped at his China tea. 'Tell me when.'

A red bus moved slowly past, blocking their view. When they could see the steps again, Denny was coming down them, holding the hand-rail. She moved to one side, glanced down the street and lit a cigarette. She stifled a cough, stepped back to lean against the building and took in another mouthful of smoke. Then she dropped the cigarette and ground it out. Ade saw she was wearing a navy blue duffle coat against the cold.

'She ain't used to smoking,' said Paul.

'Never has, all the time I've known her.'

Denny shook the cigarette packet and dropped it. She looked both ways up and down the street and turned to go up the steps.

'Now,' said Ade. 'Don't attract attention.'

There was a burst of sound as the door opened and she saw Paul dart across the road, dodging a cycle courier on a fixed wheel bike, and take up a position just next to the tax office entrance where Denny had been standing. *So far so good*, she thought. Paul crouched down, fiddled with a shoelace and swept his arm out sideways and down. Then he stood up, and walked straight into a bulky figure with a grey overcoat folded neatly over his arm, a man who had been pacing slowly along the edge of the pavement. It was the same man who'd blocked Ade's way when she came out of the tube station. *Is that what he does all day? Get in people's way?* The man was shouting at Paul, she could see his mouth opening. He'd dropped a large, briefcase with heavy straps.

Paul picked up the briefcase and offered it to him, nodding. Then he ducked his head, slipped under the man's arm and was across the road and behind a delivery truck. Ade saw the man standing on the pavement staring round. People were queued up, trying to get past him. A moment later Paul was in the chair opposite her and the cigarette box was on the table.

Ade flipped back the lid and glanced at the writing inside.

'You done good,' she said.

She squeezed Paul's hand. His eyes sparkled.

26

'Quiet neighbourhood,' said Paul, looking down the tree-lined street and up at the 1930s block of flats – red brick façade with cream edging, flat roof, and metal framed windows. 'Too far out for me.'

Ade could see a car full of school-kids manoeuvring into a drive in the distance, otherwise there didn't seem to be anyone about, though it was only half-past four. She looked at the keypad by the brown panelled front door, selected a button and pushed. A woman answered: 'Hello?'

'Jessica Dean?' said Ade. 'Can I talk to you?'

'Who's that?'

'My name's Adeline Corey, we met at the office. I introduced myself. I'm the tax inspector.'

'I don't think Mr Webster would like me to talk to the tax people.'

'It's important, it's about Mr Webster. Don't you remember: we talked, you gave me a pen? A Christmas present?' She held the pen up to the security camera. 'I've come to say thanks. And we want to help you.'

After a moment the door buzzed.

Ade was impressed by the neatness of the flat. Someone had just polished the coffee table. There was a fragrance in the air she didn't recognise. Expensive. The sofa looked brand new. Jessica motioned them to it and then sat opposite them, her knees neatly together. She wore smartly-pressed jeans and a silk shirt, her hair back in an Alice-band. She stared at Paul, who hunched down, his hands folded into his lap, making himself as small as possible.

'How can I help you?'

There was a firmness in her voice that Ade hadn't expected. 'Mr Webster is, as you know, a successful businessman,' she said. 'His business is tax avoidance. He cheats the Revenue and he helps other people cheat the Revenue.'

Jessica pushed a lock of hair behind her ear.

'And…?'

'You were aware of that?'

'Of course. I don't think you understand. I don't have money, but I'm bright and I work hard. I got a scholarship to Kings College School. I've got a first in Economics from Bristol University. I'm temping to finance my MSc, so I can start my real career. Acquisitions and mergers, that's what I'll be doing in two years' time. I know exactly what goes on in the city. I can see who comes to that office and how they behave.'

'Tax evasion is a crime. More importantly, it takes money away from the state – that's you and me. We can't have old-age pensions, we can't have hospitals, we can't have schools, all those things, unless people like Webster pay their tax. You know that.'

'Yes. It's unfortunate but that's how it is. People are always going to fiddle tax if they can. Webster is not a pleasant person,' she smiled, 'but I need the cash and I handle him. Now, if that's all you wanted to tell me…'

'Forget all that. S'not about tax.' Paul spoke for the first time.

'I'm sorry?' said Jessica.

Paul leaned towards her, Ade saw how his dark eyes were fixed on hers. 'He's a pig.'

'Of course. Don't forget I work in that office.' Jessica gave a little laugh. 'They're like that, most of them, those city types.'

'He don't respect women,' said Paul with a stubborn note to his voice.

He took the mobile phone out of his pocket, held it up to her and tapped "Play". The screen showed a street, after dark, light spilling out from a hotel entrance. A limousine drew up and the chauffeur opened the passenger door. A stout bear-like man in an overcoat, hatless, got out and turned to help another passenger, a young woman with strikingly long dark hair, dressed in a tight black dress. The man said something they couldn't catch and she giggled, ducking her head. He held her close against him as they mounted the steps. The porter held the door and the light illuminated their faces: Rex Webster and a young woman who couldn't have been more than eighteen. The woman stared straight at the camera and Ade was suddenly reminded of the homeless woman in the red anorak she'd talked to near the Monument the morning that she'd gone looking for Paul.

Jessica nodded.

'I suppose I'm supposed to burst into tears and say "But he...he promised!" with my eyes wide open and my hand to my mouth like a character in a Mills and Boon novel. Yes, I know he's a pig. And I don't think much of Mills and Boon novels.'

'We can show you some more film if you like. Different women, of course. Didn't take long to get the pictures.'

'No thanks.'

'You can help us,' said Ade. *Everything was going in the wrong direction.* 'You know he's a tax cheat, you know he's a pig. We'd like you to help us get into his office, so we can get the evidence and tell everyone what he's really like.'

'I'm sorry, I'm not likely to do that. It's the City, it's the richest and most exciting place on the planet.' Jessica spread her hands as if she was trying to explain something. 'Listen. You don't understand, not really. It isn't just money. It's the glamour of it, the power, being able to do anything you want. Anything at all, if you have enough of it.'

She looked at Ade then Paul, then back at Ade. 'You're either on the inside or the outside. I intend to be on the inside. It's my future.'

'I hope you never need an ambulance.'

'I'll buy one.'

Ade stared at Jessica. What would Morwen have said? The sound of clapping cut across the silence. Paul clasped his hands and grinned at them.

'You're smart, girl, and you're confident, just like Webster and all those clever people he knows. You've missed the main thing. You want a career with that lot. Lots of money. Never have to worry about anyone else. Good luck. How you going to get it? You're a woman. You've seen what they think of women. They ain't your friends. You can have as many first class degrees as you like, people like Webster'll always think you're their doormat.' He stood up and strode to the door. 'Come on Ade, there must be another way to do this.'

'He's right, isn't he?' said Ade softly. 'Webster and his friends, they'll use you, but they'll never like you. And you'll never be able to trust them.'

She could play the trump card now. *Did you know he tried to rape me? Do you know that's who he is?* She could say that in a gentle reasonable voice with her eyes on Jessica's. And what would happen? Would those lovely cornflower blue eyes widen, would she say, 'That's so awful, that's terrible?' Would she clutch at Ade's wrist?

Ade couldn't bear that. She couldn't bear the other Jessica either, the one that knew she could take on the city and win, because her sort of people always won, who'd look at her and pause a moment, before saying:

'That's bad, but you knew he was like that, but how did you ever get into that kind of situation with him? And yes, the City is my future and it won't be easy. I'll look pretty in their office and I'll fight and I'll win because I'm sharper than they are and I'm tougher than they are, and I can handle them.'

She stood up. 'Goodbye,' she said.

Jessica sat there. After a moment she touched Ade's sleeve, said 'No, wait a moment,' and scribbled something on the cover of a magazine and tore it off.

'Access code, for the door.'

'Thanks. And the computer?'

Jessica sat there as if she hadn't heard her. Ade found she could hardly breathe.

'OK.'

She wrote rapidly on the paper and handed it to Ade.

27

It was six-thirty and the street was crowded with people. Christmas was in full swing. An office party, all drink and laughter and outrageous dresses and silly hats, spilled out of the pub in front of them.

'Gangway!' shouted a young man in shirtsleeves, his face flushed, and pushed between them. *So much for the vampire scare,* thought Ade. *They've got short memories in the city.* She glanced round then peered at the key-pad by the plate glass door with "Webster House" in polished steel capitals on the stone-work above it.

Paul stood next to her, shielding what she was doing from the street. The door buzzed and swung open. She led the way across the thick carpet of the outer office. She could hear the hum of a vacuum cleaner somewhere else in the building, but this floor seemed to be deserted.

'How do we get into Webster's office?'

'There must be spare keys somewhere.'

Paul was looking through the drawers of the outer office desk.

'Here we are.'

There was something so comical about him, stood there in the scruffy jacket he always wore against the immaculate office décor, with a Jeff Wall painting beside him, a bunch of keys dangling from his hand and a grin across his face, that Ade nearly burst out laughing.

The lock clicked open at the third key. She smelled the air. This was Webster's place. *I hate you,* she thought, *and we're going to put you out of business.*

She looked across at the mahogany partner's desk, the black leather executive chair behind it, the guest chairs in front and the bookcase to one side, all illuminated by the light from the street streaming up through the picture window. A computer screen and keyboard were set into the desk, next to a blotter, a matching metal desk set, a cylindrical steel ruler and a miniature antique set of scales. She reached out and took one of the pens and looked at it, slim in her hand. It seemed such a small thing, so perfectly made.

'What you got?' said Paul.

Ade sat down on Webster's chair, tapped in the password and started to work through the spreadsheets, all neatly ordered, all stacked on top of each other, reaching down to the next level of transactions and the next. It all seemed familiar to her, she found she could see the pattern as soon as she looked at it. She'd looked down on it in her dream, seen it all, taken it in, grasped it, how it all linked together, how it worked.

She flicked to the layer underneath, following the trail outside the office, the network of buying and selling, trading and dealing, linking up across the city, flipping backwards and forwards, all the streams running in, the torrent of money surging, swelling, dividing and merging again, a river crashing round a rock. Then it flowed outside London, outside the UK, cascading across Europe through Russia and Singapore and Hong Kong. She lost it, then she picked it up again, in and out of Ireland, back through the Netherlands, to another Irish company and – she leaned forward to make sure – out to the Caymans and back. *We've got him. The profit's all made here, but it's shifted out there. But how does the money come back and where does it go when it gets here?* She checked through the links twice but the trail ran dry.

It was obvious when you thought about it. Webster didn't shift his money around just to bury it away in a tax-haven somewhere. He made his money in the city and he sent it though a dizzying chain of trades and contracts round in a gigantic circle and back where it started. Then he could pay everyone back. It didn't come back through all the secret connections, it came back as the profits of legitimate trading, nothing to do with business in the City subject to UK tax, but financial services off in the Caymans, insurance in Singapore, property development in Hong Kong. A lot of financial services, all based out in the Caymans, and that's overseas, not subject to UK law and paying precious little tax out there.

She took the flash drive out of her pocket, pushed it into the slot and tapped a few more keys. The green bar flashed up on the screen, slowly diminishing from one end: six minutes to download. *It's a huge file, everything I need, the whole bloody lot.*

'Everything OK?' Paul stood next to her, staring at the numbers on the screen. She looked up at his face, ghostly in the pale light.

'Better.' She found his hand and gripped it. He stood next to her in silence, watching the bar. Five and a half minutes, five minutes, four and a half minutes.

She gave a start at the noise of a key scraping at the lock of the outer office. 'Quiet, someone's coming.'

Paul shut the door between the inner and the outer office and stood behind it, holding onto the handle.

She found her chest tightening, her hands curling into fists. She breathed out and turned to the computer. The faintest of pings. The file was transferred. He mouthed the word 'Webster!' She pointed to the screen. 'One more thing.' She nursed her hatred. *Soon, very soon.*

She tapped at the keyboard: the addresses of everyone she could think of, the FT, press agencies, Channel 4, an academic she knew at LSE, a few think tanks, a couple of MPs, she had them all ready. Now, upload and send. The bar appeared; *it'll take time to attach.* She slipped the flash drive into her pocket and prayed Webster had the bandwidth.

She heard Webster fumbling at the door handle. Paul wrenched the door open. Webster stood there, dressed in an Armani overcoat, silk scarf, thick leather gloves, a mobile in his hand, his eyes open wide in surprise.

Paul bellowed 'Get out!' and ran at him, head down. He wrapped his arms round Webster's body and kicked at his shin. Webster grunted, dropped the mobile and shook Paul off. He was so much bigger than Paul, so much stronger.

'Who the hell are you?' he shouted.

He shoved Paul away and punched him hard on the side of the head, so that he fell backwards against the wall. Then he saw Ade framed in the doorway to his office, and spoke in his normal confident tones. 'You? What are you doing here? I paid you off, remember?'

'Doing my job, Mr Webster.'

Her heart was pounding. She hoped her voice sounded firm. The anger was tight, compacted, something you could hold in your hand, like a grenade.

'So I didn't pay enough?'

'Too late for that. I've just emailed your spreadsheets to everyone I can think of. If I were you I'd start running. Someplace there's no extradition.'

Webster took a pace towards her. A grin spread across his face, he chuckled and gave a great guffaw of laughter. She could smell the whisky on his breath. Her hand was in her pocket, the metal of the pen cold against her fingers.

'Oh, my dear. You're such an idealist. It would have been so good to… What do you think is going to happen?'

Ade squared her shoulders. She fixed her mind on the bar on the computer screen, the scale inching slowly, inexorably, left to right. She tried not to look at Paul, who was pulling himself to his feet, shaking his head from side to side, edging silently behind Webster.

'You are going to gaol for fraud. For a very long time.'

'Oh really. Grow up. So who's going to prosecute? City of London Fraud Squad? You think so? No, it'll be the Commissioners for me, keep it in the family. My people will tie them up in knots so tight they'll have to come to a settlement or they'll never get free again. Lucky if they get ten percent. You know what? I'll put that down as a business expense.'

'This isn't going through formal channels. I'm not with the Revenue anymore.'

'Ah. I see. I suppose what you really want is a bit of the action. Same as everyone else.'

He slapped his hands together.

'Why not? You're sharp: join the team.'

'You missed the point. I've emailed your spreadsheets to the BBC, every journalist I've ever heard of, so they all know how you work. This isn't just your friends slapping you on the wrist. You're going to be front-page news tomorrow: "The man who steals your money".'

She stepped sideways. The green bar reached the side of the screen and she heard the noise, the faintest of beeps, like a mobile getting a text in the next room. Webster took a step forward, hesitated and bit at the thumb of his gloved hand.

'You don't give up, do you? You've no idea what you're dealing with. Open that drawer.' He glanced at Paul. 'Don't try anything, you. I can deal with you.'

Paul stood there, looking from Ade to Webster and back.

'It's OK,' she said. 'Webster's finished anyway.'

Webster rummaged in his trouser pocket, took out a small key and tossed it to her. The drawer was heavy and she had to tug at it. It was crammed full of fifty-pound notes, stacked in neat bundles. Paul started giggling and stuck his hand into his mouth, but he couldn't stop.

'That's who I am,' said Webster. 'And what are you?'

Ade thrust her hand into the drawer, feeling the paper stiff against her, spread her fingers and forced her hand upwards so that a cloud of notes erupted, fanning out and falling, swaying like russet-coloured leaves to the carpet. She felt his fist on her, coarse in the leather glove. There was something so comfortable, so self-assured about his voice. She froze in his grip. The pen was cold as hail-stones on her fingers and something else, thin and hard, against it. She ran her finger gently over it. The shattered watch.

'You're a fool,' he said. 'Do you think it's just me? We run this country, the real people, the people with money. Do you think any of us want all this in the newspapers? Let's go and get a meal. You could enjoy yourself if you'd just let go.' He was smiling at her. 'The runt can clear up.'

The ice in her chest burst apart. She whirled round, grabbed his hand, ripped off the glove, and sank her teeth into his thumb. She felt them grate and skid on the bone. He screamed and staggered backwards. She spat the taste of iron out of her mouth.

She threw the watch down on the floor in front of him.

'Franck Muller. Remember that, you bastard?'

Webster gaped at her, his face white. She had the pen gripped in her hand like a dagger.

'You want to know what was in your neck that night? You want to know who put it there? When you were on your face in the mud, whimpering?'

The hatred blazed up like a furnace inside her and her fist stabbed up at his throat. Paul hurled himself at her, his arm outstretched. All she could feel was the blood pounding in her chest and the metal cold in her hand. She hated Webster and his sneering arrogance, his certainty that it was his world, that nothing in it could ever touch him.

Somewhere she heard Paul shouting: 'Ade! He's not worth it!' and she jerked her hand sideways. The pen skidded across Webster's throat, leaving a thin smear of blood.

'Get out!' she shouted at him. 'Get out now!'

Webster stepped back, staring at her, his right hand

cradled in his left. He turned and stumbled to the door, gave one backward glance, and was gone.

Paul had his arms round her. For a second she rested her face against his. Then she pulled free.

'That was close, that was very close. I could have done it that time.'

They heard the noise of the lift doors. She felt the hatred dulling within her. The blood throbbed in her forehead. 'Thanks Paul.'

She held him very tight. He clasped her to him then gently disengaged himself. 'We ought to slow him down. Nice steel ruler he's got. Matches the biro.'

She watched him pick it up, weigh it in his hands, nod, and move swiftly out of the room. By the time she'd caught up with him he was crouching down, levering at the lift doors.

'Give us a hand,' he said.

They got the doors half open. She saw the cables check and shudder to a halt.

'Don't think he's the kind of person who's much good at climbing up lift shafts.' Paul had the ruler jammed in place between the doors. 'He's going to have a very uncomfortable night.'

'But he's got a mobile... no he hasn't, he dropped it.'

Paul stamped on the phone and scooped up the pieces. 'In the river, I guess.'

'So maybe we win something after all.'

He had his arm round her. 'Guess we should have a look at this money.'

They stood in front of the desk, hand in hand, gazing down at the neatly stacked notes, the moonlight streaming down on them through the window.

'Enough here to put a lot of people who need it into housing.'

'No. It would be nice, but that's not who we are.' She picked up one of the bundles of notes. 'That'll do, we can do something with this. Leave the rest.'

She was still breathing hard, like she'd been running.

As they pushed through the double doors at the foot of the stairs into the lobby they heard a loud buzzing. A light was blinking in the shadows behind the reception desk. They crossed over.

'Receptionist does the switchboard. It's the lift emergency line. Guess it goes through to a call centre if no-one answers.'

'Suppose so.'

Paul glanced at the plate glass window, took hold of the metal chair, and swung it over his head to smash it down on the computer-switchboard. Ade reached past him, picked up the handset and placed it on the counter. The buzzing stopped. He hesitated a moment and put the chair back on the floor. They could hear Webster's voice:

'Is that Emergencies? I'm stuck in a lift in the Webster Building. Get me out of here. I want you here now.'

'Yeah,' Paul picked up the receiver. 'It ain't the Hong Kong Chinese Laundry. Buy your way out of that one.' He reached down the side of the switchboard and jerked at the phone-cord, snapping it.

Ade had her fist jammed in her mouth.

He looked up at her.

'Tax-woman and Robyn.'

She loved him.

28

Ade stood on London Bridge with Paul beside her, looking up at the night sky. *It must be nearly nine o'clock,* she thought. They'd been walking idly along by the river, just listening to the noises of the city, the rush of the water, the people chattering happily around them, the traffic on the Embankment across the water, the lights gleaming everywhere.

There didn't seem to be anything to do. The news was out, somewhere out there. Maybe the police would come after them for breaking and entering or criminal damage to lift doors or touching Webster's computer or something, or maybe they'd be too busy. Maybe Webster would have the Fraud Squad round with Fleet Street camped outside his Sloane Square mansion and all his business associates explaining how they never knew what he was up to.

The moon had come out from behind the cloud now and was lighting up the buildings all round them. London, the greatest city in Europe. So many people, from every country, speaking every language in the world. All pursuing their own lives, chasing their own dreams. All needing a government that worked, buses, drains, police, fire engines, street lighting, doctors, day nurseries, clean water, law courts, ambulances, schools, everything you couldn't have without tax, everything she worked for, keeping the city alive.

Her phone buzzed.

'Marcus Robbins, BBC News here.'

'Sorry?' She was instantly alert. Marcus Robbins was the lead for the main BBC evening news programme. He had a soft compelling voice which hardened the instant he found a weakness in one of the people he talked to so politely in front of an audience of ten million.

'I'd like you to help us. We're doing a discussion on taxation and the City this evening. It'll be the Chancellor, CI Mayland from the City of London police and, I very much hope, you. Do say you'll be able to come.'

'But...why me?'

'One of my assistants just picked up something from the FT website. You're their lead story, all about tax and city corruption. They're running with the Institute of Director's line that it's the Revenue harassing reputable businesses. Our angle's going to be tax fraud. The fat cats who don't pay what they should, so the rest of us have to stump up even more.' His voice softened. 'The tax inspectors who perform a vital public service tracking them down. The Revenue won't speak to us. Everything's confidential. We understand you're one of their leading experts and that you're now free-lance. We're relying on you.'

She heard a voice in the background, but she couldn't make out the words. She stared out across the dark band of the river to the towers of Blackfriars Station and the dome of St Paul's, weightless in the moonlight. She tried to gather her thoughts.

'You'll have the Chancellor and a senior City of London police officer... and me?'

'Yes. They're there because we have questions we want to put to them. You're there because you're the human face of taxation. I'm right, aren't I? You're the one who tracks down the tax cheats? I'm going to have to go in a second.'

She watched a couple in the street, arm in arm, window-shopping, the man pointing at something and the woman laughing.

'Yes, I'll do it.'

'Thank you.' He sounded delighted. 'Broadcasting House, 9.30pm, ask for me. Don't be late. We pay expenses.'

The elation rushed back. She clasped Paul to her.

'Webster's wrong, it's out there. I'm on TV, we'll make sure everyone knows about this.'

'That's brilliant. Number one.'

29

Twenty minutes later they were pushing open the swing doors of Broadcasting House. One of the receptionists, a pleasant-faced older woman with reddish hair and dimpled cheeks, looked up and caught her eye. Just then Paul's phone jingled. She walked toward the reception desk. She could hear Paul's voice behind her: 'Nadia? What's up?'

The older woman rose and came round the end of the desk, her hand outstretched. 'You must be Ms Corey. We're delighted you could come. I'm to take you straight up.'

Ade looked back at Paul.

'I gotta go. There's something happening at the house. Nadia wouldn't say what. I'll call you.' He was rubbing at the side of his face. 'I never heard her like this.'

The woman had a hand on Ade's arm, just above the elbow.

'We do need you now,' she said. 'You're the main item.'

Ade stood there a moment longer. 'It's a big chance. I'll see you soon.'

Four young men with identical suits and instrument cases strode past, talking loudly. Paul hugged her. 'Good luck,' he whispered his mouth close to her ear. 'Superhero.'

He turned and was gone.

The woman from reception led Ade up a flight of stairs, through swing doors and into a darkened space, where everything sounded muffled and none of the technicians looked up at her. She didn't recognise either of the two people sitting in the pool of light at the far end of the studio, chatting to each other, one in a wheelchair, the other in a leather armchair. The woman ushered her forward, then smiled and turned to go. The lights glared bright in her face. Someone clipped a microphone to her lapel, tapped it and nodded. Another assistant gestured her to the third chair, smiled cordially at all three of them and glanced at a sheaf of papers.

'Mr Robbins will be here shortly. He's asked me to say how pleased he is you could come in at such short notice.'

A middle-aged man with neatly trimmed hair and formidable black-framed glasses leaned across the arm of the wheelchair to shake Ade's hand.

'Chancellor Spalden regrets he is unable to attend this evening. He is needed in the House. I am his assistant in these matters,' he said smoothly. 'Christian Mitchkin.'

'Of course. And I represent the City of London police,' said the young black woman on Ade's right. 'Emily Stonepan. We felt it better to have a communications expert on the programme.'

She had a firm hand shake, a warm smile and guarded eyes. *When were you last on the beat?* thought Ade.

'I'm Adeline Corey,' she said. 'Ex-Revenue.'

The other two gazed at her a moment longer, as if to fix her face in their memories, then turned away to resume their conversation. The young woman checked her clipboard and turned to Ade.

'You're able to talk about the day-to-day practice of tax-gathering in the City?'

'Yes. But aren't we here to discuss the breaking news? Tax fraud on a massive scale? How it means ordinary people have to pay more?'

'Tax avoidance,' said the assistant. 'That's been done to death and there's never any proof. We want to stress the law and order angle.'

'But…'

'Here's Mr Robbins.'

Mr Robbins was much shorter than Ade had expected and more genial. He had the face of a matinee idol, the make-up round his right eye slightly smudged. His smile included all of them.

'Sorry, things are happening very fast. Everyone ready? Right, let's go. We've a short film to start with.'

The film on the monitor in front of them set stills of Webster's bandaged face against shots of City of London police patrolling the financial district: two Bobbies on glossy black horses moving down Threadneedle Street; an officer with a machine pistol slung over his shoulder scanning the crowd outside Bank tube station. Newspaper headlines were edited in: "City Vampire Strikes!"; "Muggings Up in the Square Mile"; "Tax Panic Grips City".

Ade was sure she recognised one shot from the Occupy St Paul's campaign four years ago: a line of police holding their ground against waves of demonstrators with make-shift banners. She felt uneasy. The film finished with the empty street in the early evening, the camera panning up to the full moon. The commentator spoke rapidly: 'Unprecedented scenes in the city earlier this week.

New aggressive Revenue tactics combined with the City Vampire scare have led to a tax bonanza as many firms meet tax demands without challenging them: a field day for the bureaucrats. One respected MP refers to "a serious error of judgement by officialdom."

Marcus Robbins started speaking. 'In the studio to discuss this we have Christian Mitchkin from the Treasury, Emily Stonepan from the City of London police and Adeline Corey, ex-Revenue. Mr Mitchkin, what's the Treasury's view of this?

Mitchkin smiled into the camera, his hands spread wide: 'All this was quite unexpected and we're as much in the dark as anyone else. Thank goodness the panic, for that's what it was, is now over. The city is one of Britain's greatest institutions. It thrives on stability. By next week all this will be forgotten. Of course, the Treasury is always pleased to receive more tax, but we do have a concern about business confidence.'

'You're pleased you say? Isn't that a little heartless? Mr Webster was attacked by someone masquerading as a vampire. You might call it a terror attack. He spent the night in hospital.'

'Naturally…'

'You're missing the point,' Ade broke in. 'Now we know how much tax these firms can really afford to pay. They'll never be able to plead for lower settlements again.'

All three faces swung to confront her.

'I don't think that follows,' said Mitchkin.

Robbins frowned. 'I'll come to the Revenue viewpoint in a moment. Now Ms Stonepan, the law and order aspect is central to this.'

'Yes and thank you for asking me onto your programme. This all stems from an attack on a respected businessman. It's good news that Mr Webster is fully recovered. We in the City of London police force take such things very seriously. We have tripled patrols in the city and are providing personal protection for some prominent figures. We wish to reassure the business community that London is now back to business as normal.'

'I'm sure everyone is glad to hear that. Now, Ms Corey, you've made the point about exceptional tax yields, under considerable duress, it must be said.' He raised an eyebrow. 'Do you think the Revenue's practice in retaining these payments is defensible?'

'Of course. But what is all this about "respected business people"? We all know that the City of London arranges its affairs to cheat the rest of us: offshoring profits, inflating expenses, in some cases preparing one set of books for the Revenue and one for the shareholders – and a different one for the Cayman Islands. These people don't pay their fair share so the rest of us have to pay more.'

'That's an assumption. City firms cannot afford to risk their reputation.'

'Haven't you seen the *Financial Times*? The lead on their website is about Webster's companies and what they do to cheat the government – that's us – out of tax.' She addressed the camera directly. 'Don't you understand? It's our pockets they've got their grubby fingers in – all of you out there watching.'

She thought she was doing rather well. Robbins made a sign with his left hand. The camera swung away from her. His face in close-up appeared in front of her on the monitor. He looked shocked.

'This programme would wish to dissociate itself from any unproven innuendo of wrong-doing. The paper mentioned took down that page almost immediately it was produced and has published a full apology. I understand an urgent injunction was raised by a very distinguished city law firm and approved almost immediately. The Revenue appears to be in a very difficult position.'

The camera panned back to the group. Stonepan smiled at the others. 'Let's not prejudge the issues. We have to be careful about these allegations. I'm sure we've all heard newspaper stories like this before.' She laid a hand on Ade's sleeve. 'Scare stories. We cannot take any of these allegations seriously until they are proven before the Commissioners. Surely you must be aware of that as a Revenue employee?'

Ade stared at her, dumbfounded. 'I resigned from the Revenue three days ago.'

'Ah,' said Stonepan and turned back to Mitchkin.

Robbins was talking directly to the camera.

'So there you have it. Is the Revenue out of control? Are some of our oldest-established businesses under attack? And that's all we've got time for. Thank you to our panel. And now a report on the homeless crisis.'

The light on the camera blinked off. He swung round to confront Ade: 'What on earth are you playing at? You want to go through the courts for slander, don't drag this programme in with you. You saw what happened to the FT when they started attacking Webster. You know how much that will cost them?'

Mitchkin joined in, in his slow smooth voice: 'You must know that we all depend on the City of London. It never helps to rock the boat. We must nurture the jewels in our crown. A few rotten apples in every barrel.'

Ade stood up. She felt stifled. 'You just got the world record for clichés. And you ignore everything that's happening all round us. And you call this justice?'

'But nothing much is happening,' said Stonepan. 'People always want to pick at anyone who's a success. That injunction shut the FT story down pretty sharpish. It's business as usual, I'm afraid.'

She smiled. *You spend a lot of time smiling,* thought Ade. *I guess you get paid for it.* She turned and strode across the studio. In front of her a monitor was showing footage of helmeted police on horses charging an Occupy demonstration led by a burly young woman with a home-made placard reading 'Homes not Profits' in red and black felt-tip. The camera switched to a demonstrator, her arms wrapped round her head, trying to make herself as small as she could, as a policeman swung back his baton.

The film cut to a senior officer, silver braid on his cap and his shoulders, in close-up. He spoke in a gentle authoritative voice: 'Homelessness in a city as rich as London is primarily a law and order problem. We must maintain firm control. My officers protect the rights of honest citizens. We have dealt with rioters and hooligans as they deserve. I'm delighted to say that the magistrates back us up ...'

Ade felt the anger swelling up within her, filling her chest, her breath harsh in her throat. She looked back at Stonepan and Mitchkin chatting together now the camera was off them, his hand on her shoulder. Robbins crossed in front of her, followed by the assistant with the papers. She seized him by the shoulder and spun him round like a child.

'What the hell's going on? Your job is to tell people the truth.'

The assistant took a pace backwards. Ade jabbed a finger at Robbins. 'Listen to me! Webster Consulting are running a major tax fraud involving dozens of top city firms. The evidence is all out there. We put Webster's accounts on the internet, all of them, including the spreadsheets he keeps hidden. You're supposed to be a journalist – check them out for yourself.'

Someone grabbed at her arm from behind and pulled her away. Robbins stood staring at her, his face unnaturally white, brushing at his sleeve with his free hand. 'You're not doing your own cause much good,' he said and nodded to someone behind her. 'Put her out.'

Ade felt herself taken firmly by the arm and half marched, half escorted through the studio exit and down a concrete corridor. She rounded another corner and came up against a steel door, labelled "fire exit". The security guard pulled the door open and stood there blocking her way back into the building. He was grey haired and no taller than she was, but muscular, with a face as red as a boiled ham.

'You want to pick on someone your own size? Thought not. Now get lost.'

He slammed the door shut in her face. Her foot caught against something and she staggered across an alley and found herself leaning against dirty brick-work. The blank stone wall of the television building reached up in front of her. The alley stank of dog pee and car fumes and bad air. A yellow light filtered down from uncurtained metal windows somewhere above her. *Webster's right,* she thought, *money always wins. I let you down, Paul. And you, Morwen. And you, Denny. And I still hate Webster.*

She stood there, her hand on the wall, feeling in her pocket for her phone. There didn't seem to be much point in moving.

30

Ade stood in the kitchen of the squat, her arms round Paul, holding him tight against her. She kissed him. It didn't go away, it was still there inside her, the hatred she felt for them all, and her failure.

'I knew it was going to go wrong, soon as they played that film, but I couldn't stop it.'

'Bastards. They're all in it together.' His eyes glinted. 'Listen, you did the very best you could, everyone thinks so, we all think so, all of us.'

He felt so vulnerable in her arms. He was on her side, he always had been.

'I hate them.' She kissed him again. There were just the two of them. They had to make it work. 'I guess we've got some money out of it all. They can't stop us using that. And it's over, and I lost my job. And I've got you.'

'Yeah, and I've got you. And we don't have to think about Webster ever again.'

He paused.

'There's something else, why Nadia needed me here. Someone I helped once when I was in Haringey. She's in trouble, she needed me and she came here. Easiest if Nadia explains – they're in the front room. Best I don't go in just now.'

He pointed to a door leading off the hallway. Ade pushed it open, and found herself in a smaller room, uncarpeted and lit by an old standard lamp without a shade. A woman was seated on the sofa opposite. She had a beaten look about her, as if she was used to failure. Ade saw there was a child on her lap, a girl, perhaps seven years old, neatly dressed, her hair in plaits and a stud in her ear. The child had her head down and the woman was holding her tight against her. Nadia was next to them, bent over them with her arms round them. Ade noticed the clean new bandage wrapped round her hand.

The woman looked up over the child's shoulder and Ade glimpsed slate-blue eyes. She knew she'd never seen her before but in that instant her heart went out to her. The woman looked down at the child.

'I ain't never going back,' she said. 'You can't make me. I ain't.' There was a note of sullen triumph in her voice.

'Ade! I'm so glad you're here,' said Nadia. 'Close the door.'

'But Paul…?'

'He ain't coming in?'

The woman on the sofa clasped the child to her more firmly, rocking her from side to side. The child whimpered. She looked up. Ade could see her she was terrified.

'She don't like men, she gets upset,' said the woman.

'He's OK. He came back when I asked him to help us. But he can't come in, not yet,' said Nadia to the girl. 'We won't let him.'

Ade shut the door behind her. 'What's happening? Can I help?'

'This is Ade,' said Nadia to the woman. 'She's our

friend.' She motioned to Ade to come nearer. 'Is it OK if she comes in? She wants to help us.'

'She's not going to let him in, is she?'

'No, I promise,' said Ade.

The woman looked up at her again. She seemed to relax.

'This is Gemma,' Nadia said, 'and this is Amy, her daughter.'

'Pleased to meet you, Gemma.' *I have to be very careful here.* 'Can I sit down?'

'Alright. Say "Hello", Amy.'

'Hello,' mumbled Amy. 'You going to help us?'

'Gemma lost her home,' said Nadia. 'She found out about us. She came here 'cos of Paul. Then Amy got upset.'

Gemma leaned forward slightly as if challenging them. 'Didn't lose it. I left. I had to, 'cos of her,' she clasped Amy tighter. 'Got nowhere else to go.'

'What about the council?' asked Ade. 'They have to help you. You've got a little one.'

'Bloody council, no use to anyone, they put the flat in his name, didn't they?'

'I don't understand.' Ade glanced at Nadia.

'I can tell Ade, can't I?' Nadia was talking to Gemma.

'Suppose. Just don't say nothing to him.' She nodded towards the door.

'It's like this. Gemma's a single parent. Paul helped her get a flat from a housing association, back in Haringey, when he was working there. She met Maxie.'

'He was alright 'til he moved in, he used to make me laugh.' Gemma sniffed. 'He went to them. Said we were a family, he'd pay the rent. He had money, they like that, housing benefit never covers the rent. I was stupid, I said it was alright. Don't tell Paul.'

'Yes,' said Nadia. 'The flat was transferred to his name. They had a row. That's when he started to hit her.'

'He was always sorry after. He said it was because he loved me. I put up with it for her sake.'

'I understand,' said Ade.

'Yeah. You ain't been there. Everyone understands, they always say that. But they don't and they don't do nothing and he'll find me. I know he will.'

'It's OK,' said Nadia. 'We will help you. Tell Ade what happened next.'

'Then he started looking at her.'

Amy looked from Ade to her mother, her eyes big with tears.

'Then he started giving her things like he never did before.'

'Ice cream,' said Amy. 'He give me ice-cream. Then he tried to hurt me. I ran off.'

'After that I wouldn't let her out of my sight. Then he said he'd pick her up from school. He kept on. That was last night. He kept saying, "Go on, I'm her daddy now, it's your fault she don't like me," and I said no, I'd pick her up like usual and he started hitting me.'

She sat there without speaking for a while, just holding the child.

'And later he hit me again and Amy was screaming and the neighbours were banging on the wall. Then he put his hand on Amy and he did it on purpose, in front of me so I could see, and I knew we had to go. So I grabbed her and we came here. And Amy don't like men, even Paul. You mustn't let him in.'

Ade realised that Amy had been crying soundlessly for some time, her body hunched down against her mother. 'He'll find me, I know he will, he said he would. You gotta take me somewhere, you gotta hide me.'

Nadia was stroking at Gemma's hair. 'It's OK,' she said. 'He's not going to come here. We won't let him.'

She looked up at Ade.

'That's why we don't let Paul in. When Amy saw him, she started screaming. We're keeping the others out of the way, Johnno's keeping an eye outside.'

Gemma crouched down. She seemed even smaller. 'You keep saying you won't let him, but he'll find us, he said he'll find me, he always finds me.'

Ade reached out and touched her arm. The two of them, Gemma and Amy looked up at her and she felt the lurch in her heart again.

'We'll take you to the council tomorrow and sort things out. Paul'll help us, I know he will. Now I'm going to get you and Amy something to eat. Nadia'll stay with you.'

It was later, when she'd brought in the sausage sandwiches and the brown sauce, that Ade learnt what it was that made her heart jolt in her breast. She watched as Gemma carefully lifted the sandwich, letting the fat soak into the bread and tilting it so the sauce didn't drip, before offering it to Amy. The child glanced up and took it, without any hesitation and started to eat, licking carefully at her lips between bites, keeping her eyes on her mother. Ade understood what it was. *The child trusts you. She just trusts you.*

I thought it was that you were like me, Gemma. If I hadn't been lucky, if it hadn't been for the college and Caroline I could have been you and that could have been my life. Now I know it's not that: seeing you there with Amy, I want to be you. I want to have someone love me like Amy loves you. She ached to put her arms round them. *I'm going to do something for you, Gemma, and for you, Amy,* she thought. *Paul'd help you if he could, but he can't, he can just help me and I'm going to do it.*

They sat on a wooden bench in the Housing Section Waiting Room, their eyes on the indicator above the counters. Gemma and Amy were in the middle, Nadia and Ade at the ends. Nadia was trying to interest Amy in a story book she'd found about a girl who could fly.

Ade felt Gemma leaning against her. Paul had told her everything, how it all worked, and she'd checked on the web. She took Gemma's hand, squeezed it and released it. Gemma looked up at her, her mouth set.

'Don't tell them where we're staying, he'll find out,' she said.

'I'll do the talking. It'll be OK.'

What else can I say? She looked round.

Lucky we were on the steps before they opened. The queue stretched beyond the benches with single people and families leaning against the wall at the back, some of them outside the door. All of them were poorly dressed, all of had the same hunched, beaten look about them, as if they didn't really expect anything. Even the children were silent. The air was dank on her skin as if the room was never properly ventilated.

The indicator buzzed and all the faces, black, brown, white, looked up.

'It's us,' Ade said and helped Gemma to her feet. Gemma's hand slipped into hers.

'I don't see what I can do for you.' The brisk young woman with neatly trimmed hair behind the counter kept her eyes on the pink cardboard file in front of her.

'Ms Derry has a ten-year-old daughter. She is without shelter and that makes her a priority case. You have an obligation to meet the housing needs of families with children. I don't need to remind you of that.' Ade spoke firmly. Nadia nodded.

'According to what you've told me, she is intentionally homeless.' The young woman smiled. Was she trying to look sympathetic or was she laughing at them? She spoke in flat unmodulated tones. 'In any case I have been instructed to inform all applicants that we simply don't have any housing available. Ms Derry was on our waiting list a year ago but I believe she moved out of our area. Where did you say you are? She can rejoin the list but I'm afraid it will take quite some time.'

She considered, her eyes on Gemma.

'What about your parents?'

'Dad's gone. Mum's in Belfast. She don't want me.'

'Ms Derry was forced out of her flat by a violent partner, who,' Ade leaned forward and lowered her voice, 'she believed would rape her daughter.'

She felt Gemma's hand tighten on hers so hard her fingers hurt. Amy was very quiet.

'That's different.' The young woman leaned forward. 'Have you complained to the police? Is there a court order? Then we might be able to do something.'

'He'd kill me if I went to the cops. They never do anything, anyway.' Gemma sounded as if she was going to cry. Ade longed to put an arm round her, to comfort her. 'Please try to understand. This young woman is in fear of violence and sexual assault on her daughter. She must be given priority.'

'I'm so sorry. I'd like to help but we just don't have any empty housing. Our budget for emergency bed and breakfast has been cut again. Next week we will be deciding which of the families currently in emergency accommodation must make alternative arrangements.'

She closed the file and laid a hand on it.

'I need something more concrete: an executed eviction notice or a court order. Without that I can do nothing. Now, there are others waiting.'

Ade flushed and took a deep breath. 'Can't you help us? Give Ms Derry and Amy something until we get the order sorted out?'

'I'm sorry. I've explained the situation.'

Ade stared at her. She spoke very softly. 'Let me ask you: Do you like your job?'

'What do you mean?'

'Do you like your job?'

The young woman's eyes flashed. 'For your information and in the interests of transparency, I hate it. I hate the council,' her voice rose, louder and harsher, 'I hate the government, I hate the cuts, I hate the people who won't pay tax.'

She was on her feet shouting over their heads: 'I hate the fact that there's never enough housing. I hate coming to work, I hate being at work, I hate the two-hour commute home to my own little flat every evening. I hate the whole bloody thing!'

Ade heard a rustle run round the waiting room, she turned and saw that everyone had their eyes fixed on her, waiting for something to happen.

'But it's no good. It's never any good. There isn't any housing. I really am sorry.' The young woman groped in her jacket pocket and pushed something towards them under the grill. It was a twenty-pound note.

'It's OK,' said Ade. 'We're going.'

31

'You can stay here for a bit,' said Ade. 'There's plenty of space, you get the bedroom. There's food in the fridge, we can go shopping after we've eaten.'

Gemma stared at her, Amy clinging to her skirt. Ade wanted to put her arms round her.

'You can't do that, it's your flat. You need it.'

'I want to do it, it's right I do it and I'm going to do it. It's not for ever. We'll work it out.'

'But it's so quiet here and there's grass outside.' Gemma looked round as if she couldn't believe her eyes. 'It's like on TV, how can I thank you? I just can't, I'll never…I can't.'

I'm going to do this. And, when everything's sorted, I'm going to get you in college.

'I want to do it… just for a bit. I might be moving out soon anyway.'

Amy looked up at her and spoke so softly she could hardly make out the words: 'You won't tell that man, will you?'

'He'll be OK, he's Paul. He helps me.'

'You won't tell him?' Her hands were fists, holding tight onto her mother's dress, her face turned into her. I'm the only one, Ade thought, just me standing between them and everything else.

'No, I won't tell him, not just now. You'll be safe here.
You'll have Christmas here, think of that. Now let's eat.'

She opened the door of the fridge.

'Look what I got.'

'She's got sausages! And chips!'

'I got ice-cream in the freezer compartment.'

It was a long time since she'd cooked a proper meal
for anyone, even if it was only sausages, beans and chips.
She took care over it, made sure she warmed the plates
and that everything was ready at just the same time. She
didn't let the others help; she said they could lay the table,
then she realised they weren't used to eating at a table. She
felt good, standing there at the stove, concentrating on
getting the sausages the right shade of brown before she
turned them. This was something she could do for them,
something she was good at.

She watched as Amy took a cautious mouthful of
ice-cream, licking it carefully from the spoon with the
tip of her tongue. Her face lit up and she smiled for the
first time. Ade got pasta, bread, marge, cheese, tinned
tomatoes, eggs, burgers, beans, red sauce, brown sauce,
more ice cream, more oven chips, pouring honey and a
magazine from the corner shop while Gemma and Amy
did the washing up.

'That must have cost you, I don't know, a lot of money,'
said Gemma, staring at the pile on the table.

'We'll sort it out later. I'm going to have to go now.
Nadia and I will be in touch very soon. We'll take you to
Women's Aid, get an injunction against that bastard, and
we'll get you back in your own flat.'

'Don't go.' Amy looked up at her with big eyes, holding

onto Gemma. 'Please. That man will come. The other one, back there.'

She huddled herself against her mother.

'She means Maxie,' said Gemma. 'She don't ever use his name.'

Ade squatted and touched Amy, but she didn't turn round. 'Trust me, Amy. I promise you he won't. I've got to sort things out. I will come back. I'll bring some more of these.'

Amy half-turned, one eye staring back at her, and Ade held out a gob-stopper. After a moment, the girl reached out for it. She inspected it, popped it in her mouth, took it out, examined it again, and put it back in. Gemma put her free arm round Ade and held her for a moment.

'See you soon,' she said. 'May God bless you.'

32

Ade leaned on the parapet opposite the Tower of London, watching the waves scudding along the river. The weather had turned and Paul had his jacket pulled tight round him. Two days to Christmas. Record takings on Oxford Street, same as last year and the year before. Ade thought of Gemma and her Christmas. It'd be a lot better than it might have been, thanks to Webster's cash. Webster was back in his tower, just the same as ever. She sent everyone the spreadsheets and his lawyers followed them up with injunctions and everyone said there was no bloody evidence. The papers were full of stories about high-handed bureaucrats and Scrooge in the Revenue, and who are the real blood-suckers. *Don't think about it.*

'Freezing,' said Paul. 'Let's walk. Nadia told me how it went at the homeless place.'

'Not good. But we handled it. Gemma's in my place now.'

He stopped and looked at her. 'But... what about you?'

'There's a sofa.'

'You're a good person.'

'Maybe I just don't like being on my own.'

'I meant it.'

He kissed her. She looked out over the river towards London Bridge. Somewhere ahead of her was the tangle of streets and the café where she'd first met him. Things happened and you hated people and you took your hate and you moulded it and shaped it and you made it into something you could use. Maybe the same applied to love?

'It's not that, is it? What you said about being on your own? You could come over to the squat.'

She smiled and pulled him to her. 'No, it's not that. It was Gemma at first, I thought if I'd not been lucky, I could have been like that, my life could have been just like her's.' She was speaking softly, her mouth very close to Paul's. 'Then I realised it was the way Amy held her. The way Amy trusted her, the only one she trusted in the world. She had something I wanted, I wanted to be her and I can't be her so I'm going to help her. That's what it is, that's why she's sleeping in my bedroom and I'm on the sofa.'

Paul stood there in her arms, not saying anything. After a while he spoke: 'That's cool.' He glanced away, over the river.

'Paul, I want to be with you. You know I do. Only, I've been through a lot. Give me time, it'll take a little time. You've been there with me, you stood by me. I love you so much.'

He smiled and blinked and said, 'I love you, Ade. Very much indeed. I want to be with you.'

'Soon.'

There was a silence between them. Ade continued: 'She's the same age I was at college. I'm going to sort things out for her, I want to. You can help me.'

'Yeah.'

His phone buzzed. He glanced at it and laughed. 'You'll like this,' he said. 'About Webster. It's all over Twitter.'

She swung round to face him. 'Not…?'

'No, they've put the lid on that. It's Jessica. Seems she thought a bit about what we said. She'd been taking notes on Webster and his friends. She put it all on Facebook. Result: she's raised her profile, Webster's missus is divorcing him and the tabloids love it: 'Sex and the City', 'Dirty Webster Taken to the Cleaners'.'

'It's not the main deal.'

'Look on the bright side. Mrs Webster wants the children and half his money and the country house and the staff and the holiday home on the Greek island and the Roller. Lots of people think the country house and the holiday home is greedy, but it's going to be messy and the papers love it. And it's having a go at how the bastards treat women. Anyway it's fun. I like a laugh.'

'You don't let things get you down do you?' She squeezed his hand.

'Got to keep going.'

'So he gets more stick for how he treats women than for all the money he's stolen in his tax fraud.'

'Maybe there's something in that. He's a bastard all round.'

Later she said: 'Sexism, publicity, just a minute, I've had an idea.'

She felt his hand stiffen in hers. 'Listening.'

'You know, I talked about welfare rights, advice, counselling, getting injunctions, taking appeals, all that kind of thing?'

'S'not easy.'

'Sure. Just thought. I could start now. With my friends in the police.'

'Where are you going?'

'Snow Hill Police Station.'

'That's City of London! Wait. I'm scared for you, let's talk this over. I'm coming with you.'

The desk sergeant knocked on the door labelled *CI Mayland, Fraud Section* and pushed it open. He stood back and nodded to Ade. Mayland was seated behind the desk, a computer to one side and her eyes on the paper file in front of her. She was eating something. Ade pushed the door to and said: 'Good afternoon.'

Mayland looked up and smiled her sympathetic smile. She slapped the file shut and, reaching down, closed a drawer, locked it and pocketed the key.

'Ms Corey! Please sit down. You told my desk officer you had some information on the Webster case. What can I do for you?'

She pressed a button on her phone and glanced at the door.

Ade sat with her hands on the table. 'Thank you for agreeing to see me.'

'I told you I wanted to help you. I really do.'

Mayland reached out to pat the back of Ade's hand. Ade put her hands in her lap. The door opened and Jones poked his lean, lantern-jawed face through the gap. 'Ma'am?'

'I've brought someone with me. My friend prefers not to discuss her business with a male officer.' Ade spoke firmly. 'Sergeant Jones could wait outside.'

Mayland looked sharply at Ade. 'I'm sorry?'

'It really does concern Mr Webster. Something you

need to know about. Sergeant Jones really should go, just for a couple of minutes.'

Mayland glanced at him and nodded. He withdrew.

'So. What do you wish to discuss?'

'There was a disagreement at Mr Webster's offices the other day. I suppose he told you about it? Mr Affarn was there. I believe Mr Webster became trapped in a lift.'

'Can't say he mentioned it. Of course, I know about the email business. I saw you make a fool of yourself on TV. I really do want to help you, but you don't make it easy. You should have thought about the injunction.'

'Easy to get injunctions when the judge went to the same college you did and so did the lawyer – and the CI of the City Fraud Squad.'

'That's just the kind of insinuation you really mustn't make in front of witnesses. But I've got a thick skin. I'm proud of being among the first women admitted to Brasenose. And I should be – only undergraduate there in my year from a state school. Did you know that? I am trying to help you, but you see the problem.'

'Let me explain. I've a friend, Ms Gemma Derry. She's part of it, I'd like to bring her in.'

'OK.'

Ade slipped outside, holding the door open. After a moment she led Amy through by the hand and, close behind her, her mother. Gemma had washed and combed her hair. Her face looked fuller, less sallow. Amy was neat as ever. Ade pulled over a chair for Gemma and she sat with Amy on her lap, her arms round her. Gemma stared at Mayland. Amy peeped over her arm, slowly gaining the courage to look round the room.

Ade sat there, facing Mayland, her chest so tight she could hardly breathe. 'Gemma and Amy Derry. Chief Inspector Mayland.'

Mayland smiled: 'So good to meet you.'

She offered her hand and Gemma took it. Amy locked her arms firmly round her mother.

'So,' said Mayland.

'Gemma and Amy have left their flat in fear of Gemma's partner, Maxie. He subjected Gemma to a regime of rape and sexual bullying. They left when he started to threaten Amy with the same. Amy doesn't like men near her. We didn't find it easy to get her to come into the station. That's why we didn't want Jones here.'

'I see.'

Mayland was looking at Gemma like she mattered, she wasn't just another minor problem in the day. Ade felt herself warming to the CI despite everything. *Not easy for a woman to make your way in the City police*, she thought.

Mayland continued, addressing Gemma: 'You are the victim of a serious crime and it is to your credit that you have come forward. We take this very seriously and we know it is very hard for you. Men like Maxie must not be tolerated. But I deal with Serious Fraud. You should be talking to my colleagues. I'll take you over, make sure they understand and that your case is handled by a woman officer.'

'Thank you. That's helpful,' said Ade. 'We need an injunction for non-molestation. Now. With powers of arrest.'

'But that will have to be a matter for a court. Not difficult if you have the evidence, but it will take a bit of time. What's all this got to do with Webster?'

Ade slid her hand into her pocket and took out a black smartphone. She laid it on the desk, screen uppermost.

'Webster. It's about how he treats women.'

Mayland glanced at Gemma and Amy, then back at Ade. 'Go on,' she said.

'Here's some film we've shot of him. There's lots more, same kind of thing.' She pressed the button and the tiny images of the fat man and the long-haired young woman in the impossibly high heels climbing the hotel steps played through.

'No one likes that kind of thing but it's not illegal, Ms Corey.'

'Bonking anything half his age, or younger. You've been in Webster's office, you've seen how he treats his secretary?'

'Yes,' said Mayland. 'Tiresome. But she hasn't complained. What's it got to do with Ms Derry?'

'Listen. He's not just in it for money or sex. It's power, it's being able to do what you like with anyone you like. With their body. Same as Maxie really. That's power. Webster treats women like he does because he can. Same as Maxie treats Gemma and Amy.'

'Don't think I don't know that. I've said I'll help Gemma. But my job is fraud. Is there anything you can tell me about Webster, anything serious?'

Ade kept her eyes fixed on Mayland's. Her heart throbbed in her chest. *You have to do this*, she thought. *It's not really for Morwen or for Gemma. It's for you.*

She spoke very softly. 'You know he tried to rape me?'

She took out the metal pen, clicked out the point and laid it on the desk. Mayland stared at her, unmoving, her face expressionless. Ade could scarcely voice the words.

'So I stabbed him in the neck with this. You remember? That night Webster was attacked on the street. When he told you he couldn't remember anything that happened. When you came to see me at the office the next day.'

She clicked the point in then out again.

'There's probably some DNA on it. And my fingerprints. So you've got me. Attempted murder. Case solved. You could have me locked up for a very long time.'

She rolled the pen towards Mayland.

'And you'd be doing just what he wants.'

The room was very quiet. Ade was hardly breathing. *Should I hold out my wrists for the cuffs? No, overdoing it.*

'So it was you. And he tried to rape you? And there are no witnesses, no real evidence? Of course not, the staff in that place know what side their bread's buttered on.' Mayland ran a hand through her hair. 'First guess is generally right.'

She reached out and picked up the pen and held it, clicking the point in and out. After a while, she took out a tissue, licked it and carefully wiped it over the pen. Then she wrapped it in the tissue, wrapped a clean tissue round it and placed the package back on the desk.

'Oh bugger,' she said. 'I've spoiled the evidence. And I've got a cold coming on too. You might as well throw that in the river.'

Ade let out her breath in one long gasp.

Mayland went on: 'You're doing this for Gemma?'

Ade nodded: 'And for Amy.'

202

'You took a big risk, coming here with that. An injunction. Why not?' Mayland pulled the keyboard towards her and tapped at it for a few minutes.

Ade leaned over to Gemma. 'It's going to be OK,' she said softly. She winked at Amy. Amy stared at her over Gemma's arm, her eyes large.

Mayland finished typing and looked up. 'That's settled. The order will be executed first thing tomorrow. If that bastard – that's a technical term used by women police officers – comes near you, dial 999 and he'll have more grief than he can imagine. Much more.'

She unlocked the desk drawer, opened it and took something out. 'Here. A couple of Mars bars. One now, one for later.' She held them out to Amy who slipped out a hand for them under her mother's arm. Gemma nudged her.

'Thank you,' said Amy. Ade reached out and picked up the package on the desk, the tissues crumpling in her hand.

Mayland grunted and turned to Ade. 'See? Maybe I'm not as bad as you think, I just like to make the thing work. Never had kids myself, no time for it. Don't expect to see you again. And you're old enough to buy your own Mars Bars.'

33

Ade loved Christmas dinner. She loved the smell of roast turkey. She loved the way the fat trickled out when you plunged the knife in. She loved the bread sauce, the stuffing, the parsnips, the roast potatoes, the gravy, the pudding, blue flames dancing round it and the sprig of holly on top, the brandy butter, the cream, the mince pies and the crackers. She loved the sherry, the white wine, the red wine and what was left of the brandy in small glasses, and the milk stout in bottles. *In some ways*, she thought, *I'm a traditionalist.*

'Not bad,' she said, wiping her mouth with the back of her hand, then stopped and used the napkin, a square of kitchen roll. 'Not bad at all.'

Gemma nodded and fanned at her face. Amy sat between them, grinning from one to the other.

'Another mince pie?' asked Ade. Amy reached out her hand then remembered and said 'Please,' and lifted her plate. Ade put the pie on it and poured thick cream over it.

'Don't know where she puts it,' said Gemma sleepily.

It was Christmas Eve, an early Christmas dinner because she'd have one with Paul and everyone at the squat, but he was a veggie, and Gemma had insisted and done most of the work. Anyway, it was best he didn't come to the flat, not just yet, not until Amy had got used to things. They'd been hard at work since breakfast, stuffing the turkey with the stuffing they'd made yesterday, getting it in the oven, then all the vegetables, potatoes first, followed by the parsnips, Brussels sprouts and carrots, then the pigs in blankets and bread sauce and everything else. They had to remember to baste every half hour, when the rich breath of the oven poured out over them and Amy had to be held back. *Good thing I know that oven,* thought Ade.

Gemma had worked out a time-table. They'd got the pudding out and ready, they'd put the mince pies on silver paper so they could warm them, they'd boiled the water and started the roast potatoes in the microwave, they'd mixed up the brandy butter and left it to coagulate, they'd studded the onion with cloves for the bread sauce (Amy had crumbled the bread, the day before) and they'd opened the red wine to let it breathe and they'd had half a glass each to try it before starting on the sherry. Amy had had coke and a half glass of wine and water with the meal. They'd do the washing up later. Much later. Maybe it would be a good chance to bring Paul over, tomorrow. He could do it while they were in the other room. She'd slip out and help him for a while.

They moved to the sitting room, Amy on the sofa and Ade in the chair opposite the TV. Gemma came in with the tea and set down the tray. Ade stared.

'More mince pies? That's stamina. I'll just have the one.'

Amy ate the mince pie as if she'd been starved. 'Is it presents now?' she asked, glancing between them.

'I suppose so,' said her mother, 'and I'm going first.'

She took Amy's hand in hers and they both looked at Ade. Ade saw how large and tender her eyes were.

'You've done so much for Amy and me, sorting out the police and the papers for the court and making us safe and everything. There's no way we could ever say thank you. It's something my Mum gave to me, God rest her soul, and I want you to have it, 'cos you're the best person I ever met. There, I've got tears in me eyes.'

She sniffed and wiped her nose and presented Ade with a large brown-paper parcel that gave against her fingers when she held it. Amy started weeping but smiling at the same time and bouncing on the sofa.

'Open it! Open it!'

Ade felt the tears coming to her own eyes. 'Thank you very much. It's been my pleasure to help, it really has.'

'Open it!'

She pulled at the paper but the sellotape bound right round it made it difficult, so she tore the wrapping all down one side and slid it off. There was a layer of tissue, then, inside it, delicate silky white material, carefully folded, with a lacy edging and little seed pearls sown on.

'You can hold it up, look,' said Gemma.

Ade found the shoulder straps. 'Oh my!'

It was a full-length white silk dress with a train and pearls. The pearls were translucent, almost glowing.

'It was my Gran's wedding dress. And my Mum's. There's a lace cap and a veil and satin slippers.'

'Oh Gemma, it's gorgeous but you can't give it to me. What about Amy when she gets married?'

Amy shivered. 'Ain't never going to get married.'

'But you might want to one day.'

Gemma rose to her feet. 'I made up my mind. Amy agrees. We want you to have it. You might need it. We want you to need it, don't we Amy?'

Ade flung her arms round both of them. They smelt of sherry and Christmas pudding and turkey and brandy butter and mince pies, sugary and aromatic and rich and spicy and everything jumbled together at once. She felt her head swimming.

'Thank you so much. I'll take very good care of it.' She folded the dress up and wrapped the tissue paper over it to protect it. 'Now I've got something for you.'

She handed Amy a neat, flat parcel in Christmas tree paper from Wilkinson's with a red ribbon. 'Thank you,' said Amy, taking it in both hands and holding it as if she were frightened of dropping it, 'thank you so much.' She carefully tore off the end and folded back the paper to display a flat grey plastic surface.

'Put it on the table and open the lid.'

Amy's eyes shone. She lifted the lid gently using both hands.

'It's from Paul and me.'

Amy snatched back her hand and put her fingers to her mouth, staring up at Ade.

'It's all right. Paul's not here. He's a friend, a good man. He wanted you to have this.'

Ade smiled at her.

'Just touch the screen. Not too hard.

After a moment Amy stretched out a hand and dabbed at the surface. The computer came to life with a synthetic fanfare and showed a screen saver of Father Christmas. She giggled.

'It's a man,' she said. 'With a beard.'

'It's Father Christmas,' said Gemma and Ade together. 'He can't touch you. There are some nice men in the world. Like Paul.'

'Suppose.'

Ade ran her finger across the screen.

'That's the art programme. Go on, make a picture, just use your fingers.'

Ade and Gemma exchanged glances over her head. Amy was drawing a horse on the screen, not too badly.

'But those things cost a fortune,' said Gemma. She had her fingers crossed.

'It's OK. Paul got it for me. He knows people, he can get things like that dead cheap. He thought Amy'd like it. He'd show her how to use it if you'll let him.'

'Now it's my present' said Amy. She went to the bedroom and came back with a roll of paper with a piece of pink ribbon tied round it. She held it out, balanced on both arms, smiling, with her lips sucked in in excitement.

'Now I wonder what this can be...' Ade made her eyes large and round. She slowly undid the ribbon then flicked open the paper so it unrolled across the coffee table and onto the floor, two metres long. 'Oh,' she said. 'Oh my. Oh Amy.'

Every square inch of the paper was covered in writing, some large, some small, some so small she couldn't read it, in black, green, yellow, brown, blue, crimson, purple, turquoise and brick red. It was written in all sorts of scripts, gothic, Arabic, modern, angular, copybook, italic, some of it horizontal, some of it vertical, at all sorts of angles, in spirals and circles and zigzags. She stared at it and read the same words over and over: 'Thank you, Ade. Thank you, Ade. Thank you, Ade.'

She wrapped an arm round Amy. 'That's wonderful, how long did it take you, it must have taken hours?'

Her other arm was round Gemma.

'She worked at it pretty well all the time, whenever you was out, I couldn't stop her.'

Amy whispered in her ear: 'I love you, Ade. Nearly as much as I love my Mummy.'

'Best Christmas I've ever had.' *I'm not just saying it, it's true.*

34

She caught sight of Paul from the far end of the street, waiting for her outside the café. He waved and started to run towards her, with the glittering Christmas decorations above him in the early evening darkness and the lights of the shops on each side. He ran clumsily, one hand behind his back. She wasn't going to run, not with that Christmas dinner inside her.

She wrapped her arms round him, her face buried in his warm hair, smelling the scent of him, then leaned back and kissed him for a long time. 'Best Christmas ever and it's getting better and better and it's not Christmas Day yet!'

She held him tight against her as they walked along the street. He squeezed her, one-armed, then brought his other arm round from behind his back. 'Here's something for you.'

He held up a bouquet of flowers, dahlias, crimson, white, orange, turquoise, their great heads glowing in the darkness. She plunged her head into them and breathed in the bouquet, rich and sumptuous.

'Dahlias – at Christmas! However did you get them?'

'I still got friends. They're for you.'

He stood there smiling at her. She had her arms round him. 'I love them.'

'There's something I've got to say to you.'

'Just a minute,' Ade gripped his hand. 'I know what I want to do. I want to be part of your homeless centre when you get it. I want to do welfare rights. I've known it ever since I was in the homeless place at the council. It's what I've always been good at, money, numbers, spreadsheets, bureaucracy, making sense of the law. I'll learn all the rules, how to deal with the system, how to fill in the forms. What works and what doesn't. I'll tell people, maybe one day I'll train others. I'll do test cases. It'll grow.'

'That's brilliant, but it ain't easy. I don't know when there'll ever be a homeless centre.'

'No reason not to keep on.'

'I think you're wonderful. And that's what I want to talk to you about.' He paused and glanced down, and took both her hands in his. 'Ade, what do you say to a Christmas wedding?'

She realised he was suddenly on his knees, on the pavement, looking up at her. 'I love you. Will you marry me?'

She looked at him for a second. She knew she needed time, there were so many things she hadn't finished, some she hadn't started. *There's never a right time.* She heard a voice inside her, drowning out all her other thoughts and she didn't know if it was Nadia, or CI Mayland, or Denny or Morwen or all of them. *Listen to your heart,* it said, *what else is there?*

He seemed so vulnerable, so incomplete, so full of life, and they'd be together and it would work, she knew it would, and she wanted it so much. She pulled him to his feet and clasped him against her.

'Yes, yes and yes! But … everything that's happened. It doesn't go away just like that. It'll take time. You know that, don't you?'

I'll always hate him, it'll be there, but you put layers round it and after a while it doesn't hurt so much. Like building a pearl.

'I'll cope. I've got issues too. But don't squeeze too tight.'

They were kissing then, again and again on the street corner. She became aware of something brushing ever so gently on her cheek, against the back of her hand.

'It's snowing!'

Fat white flakes were whirling down out of the night, gleaming in the streetlights, already beginning to settle along the pavement. She watched him put out his hand, a snowflake melting slowly against his pink palm. The snow was thicker now, muffling the noise of the city, forming a screen round them, softening the Christmas lights into a luminous haze. She shivered.

'Come on! I need sausages!'

'You've just had Christmas dinner.'

'Yeah. This is supper.'

He kissed her again.

35

Ade stared at the menu over the counter. *Black pudding today*, she thought. She'd decided to look after herself, she was going to limit it to twice a week.

It was three weeks into the New Year. She stared at the folder in front of her, the papers spilling out if it across the table. Maybe. They'd got the injunction. Maybe they could get Gemma a flat of her own. Then she and Paul…

Getting a flat out of the homeless people. It wouldn't be easy, like Paul said. He always said things like that. He was usually right. Then he went at it, anyway. He was with some of his friends from when he worked for Centre Point, in the pub. They had plans to set up a homeless centre with the money she'd got from Webster. Advice and maybe some short-term accommodation. Maybe. Get them started anyway. But there was something else she had to sort out just now.

She took a long cream envelope out of her pocket and laid it on the table in front of her. The address was typed in a faux antique copperplate script. It had come to the flat by special courier that morning, delivered by a polite young man who had been most careful to get a signature for it. She could see how Gemma had relaxed when she opened it and said it was OK, just for her, nothing to do with Maxie or the flat. They'd talked about how Amy was settling at the new school. She'd already asked if she could bring some friends back, she'd never wanted to do that before.

Ade gave a wry smile. *Want to beat the City of London and you end up doing one small good thing. Which is OK.*

Paul waved to her from the door. He was kissing her before she'd had time to rise from her seat. He sat down and immediately started talking. 'It's great. We've got the plan worked out. I'll be one of the wardens. We'll have another go at getting the money. Alex thinks he can get a meeting with this philanthropist person. We can make it work, I know we can. We're going to ask for enough to pay a worker for a year.'

'That's you.'

'Oh no. I don't take the money.'

'So how will we live?'

He shrugged.

'Find a way. Always have. Can't really look homeless people in the face if you've got a good salary can you? Look, there's these porridge pots. You just add hot water. Do you think they'd...?'

'Ask 'em. But what you said about homeless people and having a salary. Is that true?'

'It's how I feel. I'll ask about the porridge.'

'Wait, there's something else first. Listen.' She opened the envelope and slid out the sheet of thick lawyer's paper.

'"Dear Ms Corey,"' she read,

'"My client wishes you to attend in room 1.17 at the Consultancy Clinic, Harley Place, tomorrow at 3.00pm, where you will hear something to your advantage.

You are under no obligation, but we respectfully request that you accede to this invitation,

Yours faithfully,
Josiah Threadgold,
Attorney at Law."
It came yesterday.'
'You going to go?'
'Why not? Only if you'll come too. Get your porridge and eat up.'

Ade would have taken the Consultancy Clinic for a substantial private residence, with its black painted railings and white stone steps up to the front door, if she hadn't noticed the discreet brass plate screwed to the wall.

'Why's this street so quiet?' asked Paul. 'You can hear your footsteps.'

'Only residents allowed in. That's class for you.'

Ade rang the bell and a spare young man in a spotless nurse's uniform opened it. He took them in in one glance and stood there barring the entrance. 'Can I help you?'

Ade handed him the letter.

'Ah, Ms Corey. Do come in. And this is?'

'A friend,' said Ade.

The young man hesitated, then turned and led them into a hallway, past an inlaid Louis Quatorze table and up a staircase with a polished mahogany banister. He ushered them through swing doors and into a modern annex at the rear of the building. Ade caught a whiff of hospital disinfectant. She heard the sound of weeping and saw at the far end of the corridor another nurse helping a very young woman in a hospital smock through another set of doors.

The young man put out an arm to direct them onto another corridor. He halted and turned to them. 'Our client is very weak. You mustn't tire him. He requested that I give you some background information.'

He closed his eyes and opened them. Ade saw they were hazel brown.

'An unfortunate case. He collapsed at a business lunch two days ago. We brought him in and our diagnosis is, I'm very sorry to say, pancreatic degeneration. Advanced. There is little anyone can do at this stage. He wished you to know that. We are a discreet institution. You must understand that you enter on condition that none of this is ever discussed with anyone outside these walls.'

Ade nodded.

'Please sign this document.' He turned to Paul. 'And you. Remember, we have your details and will not hesitate to take action if the agreement is breached in any way whatsoever.'

He watched them sign, then carefully folded the papers and slid them into a long envelope.

'A short visit. You mustn't tire him.' He tapped on the door next to him, listened and opened it, standing back for them to enter. 'Please go in.'

Ade's first impression was of flowers, pink, yellow, red, white, in tubs and vases, the rich mingled scent everywhere in the sunlit room. The image of her mother on the trolley in the hospital corridor under the fluorescent light flashed across her mind. She looked at the figure on the bed, an old man, his cheeks sunken, his thin grey hair carefully combed back.

'You came,' he said in a thin voice. 'You...'

He paused as if it was an effort to speak. His hands lay on the white linen bedsheet. There was a drip inserted in the back of his left wrist. Wires ran towards him from a machine by the bed and disappeared under the blankets.

Ade stared at him.

'Mr Webster…'

She heard Paul mutter 'Streuth!' behind her.

Webster was speaking again, more strongly. 'Yes, didn't expect to see me like this. I suppose the young man explained.' He paused again and his eyes glittered at her.

Ade thought of the reasons why she hated him. 'I'm sorry to see you like this.'

'Doubt it.'

Some of the old arrogance was back in his face. It wasn't the cheating, it wasn't even the sexism, it was his unassailable self-assurance, the absolute confidence that he could do what he liked with money, with the law, with her body, and no-one could ever touch him. That was what she hated most about him, the certainty of power.

'I should go. You'll want to spend time with your family.'

'Hardly. At least you're not stupid.'

The fire went out of his eyes and he lay back on the pillow.

'Listen. You live once and you're dead a long time. You don't know that yet, not really. You're young.'

He paused again. She heard the breath wheezing in his throat.

'I want something.'

Ade felt Paul's hand in hers. She held it, and thought how smooth his skin was, how alive.

'You can ask.'

'I want to give you my money.'

217

Paul gave a low whistle.

'But…why?' she said.

'No one else I'm going to give it to.'

The figure on the bed seemed to contract. He started coughing, a dry retching cough. Ade released Paul's hand, took a tissue from the box on the bedside table and wiped it across Webster's lips.

'Damn flowers. Too many of them. They send you flowers, they never come and see you.' He lay there, looking up at her, gathering his strength. 'Just one condition. You build flats, lots of them. You call them the Webster Foundation. I want my name on them.' He pulled himself up on the pillows. 'I want a statue, I want my name carved in stone with a Latin inscription, I want the minister opening it, I want my name in all the papers, I want everyone to know.'

He coughed again.

'Let that damn bitch try to get her hands on the money then.'

He fell back and closed his eyes and lay without moving. Ade thought of how he looked there on the bed, shrunken, an old man, and of the face in the lift looming over her, reflected endlessly in the mirrors, of the bulk of him trapping her, his hands on her body, the roll of fat at his neck pressing against her so she could hardly breathe.

'I meant, why me? Ms Devi can set up a Foundation any day.'

The mouth twitched. She realised he was grinning at her. 'You and me. Unfinished business. Settle accounts.'

That was all it was about. The whole thing. Power.

Showing you could make someone who hated you do what you want.

The effort of talking seemed to have exhausted Webster. He lay there without moving, his eyes closed. She hated him.

'No,' she said. 'Not with your name on. There's other ways to get money.'

'Ade ...' Paul was gripping her hand so tight it hurt.

'No. Webster the great philanthropist. I can't be part of that, not after what he did. Let's go.'

Webster's eyes were open, gazing at her. He licked at his lips. 'That's it, then ... a dying man's request. I can always give it to Brasenose.'

She stood up. Bones, nothing but bones lying there in the bed and the glint of the eyes like cleft flint.

'Don't go,' he said. 'Sit down.' He coughed. 'I want to talk to you. He can go out.'

The anger blazed up in her. *The runt can clear up.*

'We're going. You want the Webster Foundation? You can do it without me. I can't pretend you didn't do what you did. I can't.'

She shoved at the door and stepped through, Paul close behind her, still talking to her, his voice urgent, but she couldn't catch the words. She didn't look back.

They pushed past the slim young man and through the double doors, Paul half-running to stay beside her, his hand curled round hers, all the way down the stairs and onto the street. She halted and swung round to face him. He rubbed at his cheek.

'You're a tough lady,' he said. 'You ever think you're too tough?'

36

Ade glanced down the empty street to Cavendish Square, a hundred yards away. Darkness had fallen and the rush hour was in full swing. A chill wind blew behind them. She put her arm round Paul, and felt him shiver. *Webster, the bastard.* He wanted to be there, in her head for ever, for ever telling her she'd done what he wanted, because he wanted her to.

'Christ, you're cold. We'll get you a decent coat. Christmas present, my treat, Oxford Street. Beats me why you've never got one before.'

Paul looked at her with his dark eyes and suddenly she didn't know what he was thinking. After a few moments he said 'That's easy. Reminds me.'

'What do you mean?'

She was rubbing at his hand. She didn't seem able to warm him. 'No fancy coat. Reminds me of what it's like to be on the street. You don't understand.'

'Maybe I don't. I've never been homeless. But I've seen people, I've felt sorry for them, I've given them money. I've fought all my life to get the taxes to pay for a proper welfare state.'

'Them. Given them money.' His free hand was pulling at a lock of his hair. 'Them. That's the worst thing. On the street you're not a person, you're them. No-one looks at you, when someone talks to you like you're human it's a real event. There's a barrier between you and normal people and there you are, shut off, you're not part of the human race, unless they chuck you fifty pee. Like a monkey in the zoo. You're never safe, you never have a place that's your own, where you can be safe.'

She let go his hand.

'That's like me and Webster's world. Just a bit. You can never touch them; they wouldn't give the shit off their shoes for you.'

They were walking south, towards the square. Paul hunched his shoulders against the wind, his hands in his pockets.

'So that's why I don't have a coat. Makes me feel closer to the street. In the cold, on the outside.'

'Yeah. You're right, I didn't understand.'

Paul stopped and turned to face her. 'That bastard. He offered you enough cash to do something real. Millions. Tens of millions. Get people off the streets, in their own place, even if it's just overnight. I don't care what it cost you. You should've taken it.'

'You're shaking with cold. We've got to get you somewhere warm.'

'Listen to me. I could take you places you wouldn't believe existed. In this city, less than a mile from here. You go along under the bridges at the right time, you can see the security guards with fire hoses cleaning out the sleepers. Washing you out, like you're filth. Soaking you. They think it's a game. They let you get a few yards, dragging your sleeping bag, then they knock you off your feet again. Try to get warm after that.'

221

His eyes glinted with passion.

'I could take you round the night shelters when they're full and they've made the selection – selection, that's the word for it – and they shut the doors and there's the ones left outside. And anywhere warm, the police move you on, 'cos no-one wants you if you haven't got money. And you move on, and you move on and that's it. Winter, it gets bloody cold, not like it is now, real cold. When you breathe, you feel the ache in your teeth.'

He paused.

'I could take you round with the soup kitchens and I could take you into the shadows under the flyovers, in the parks, at the back of the demolition sites. I could show you the ones that won't come out, even for free food when they haven't eaten all day. The one's who've found a place that can be theirs for the night, where they think they can be safe for a few hours, and would rather starve than see someone else take it.

You should've let him give you the money. A statue. His name carved on it. What does it matter? Get the graffiti artists onto it.'

'Maybe you don't understand what he did,' she said. 'He treated me as a thing. He made me hate him so much I wanted to kill him. That's what he did. You want me to accept that, to say, "Hey, didn't like it at the time, but it was all worth it?"'

They stood there for what seemed a long time. A long black limousine swept noiselessly past them and away toward the lights of Oxford Street.

'Yeah,' he said. 'I'm sorry. I shouldn't have said all that. It's just… being able to get Johnno and Mariska and Ilah and Nadia and even Casey and all the rest of them into proper flats for once in their lives. It's my dream.'

Ade put both her arms round him.

'I can't get you warm. I wish I could get you warm.'

'I'll be all right.'

'Come on. We're going back. You wait outside.'

37

Ade pushed open the door and the scent of the flowers hit her immediately, too sweet, too rich. He seemed to be asleep, his hands on the blankets. She gazed at the man on the bed. She understood virtually nothing about him. Power: making other people do what you want even when they hate you. To use them as things. Even when you're dead. She gripped the pen in her pocket.

'You're back,' he said, without opening his eyes.

She wouldn't speak immediately. She'd take a minute. She didn't have to say it right away: *It's OK. It doesn't really matter what you did, not compared with the money you made. I've changed my mind; we'll take your money. We'll cast the statue in bronze, best quality. It'll last a thousand years, longer than the buildings. We'll do anything. We'll get the Archbishop to open it. The Queen, the Prime Minister. You were right all your life. Money's the only thing that counts. Everyone's for sale and that includes me.*

She could wait a little longer. She watched him lying there with his eyes closed, as if gathering all his strength. He coughed weakly and the cough turned into a sigh.

It was a thing that had to be done.

'I'm back,' she said. 'We've talked it over. We would like to accept the money. With gratitude.'

The eyes flickered open. 'And the conditions?'

'We accept all the conditions. There's just one thing. Paul is to be chief executive of the Foundation.'

'That idiot? What do you want him to run it for?'

There was a creaking, grating noise. The eyes glittered at her and the mouth twitched. Ade realised that Webster was laughing. The noise stopped and he sucked in a breath. The lips moved again: 'No. Not paying him. Not with my money.'

'So you don't negotiate?'

'Only to win.'

Ade rose to her feet. He seemed so small, lying there on the bed. *Maybe all you had to do was pull out one of the tubes that went into the machine, fiddle a bit with the dials, turn off the drip...* He was going to be dead a very long time and he wanted them, all of them to remember him, to remember his money. She stroked the tips of her fingers along the pen in her pocket. She remembered his face reflected endlessly in the lift, the stink of whisky on him as he loomed over her. She remembered the pen sliding into his flesh, so smoothly it seemed to need no effort at all. She thought of the homeless people huddled on the pavement in Fish Street, and Paul running towards her, shouting out 'Come on!'

She thought of Denny and her half-bottle of sweet sherry. She thought of Nadia frowning with concentration as she drew the shard of glass across her palm. She thought of Marcus Robbins spinning round when she grabbed at his shoulder. She thought of Gemma and Amy and Amy's thank-you note. Everything seemed so far away, as if she was looking at it through the wrong end of a telescope. Who the hell cared?

She remembered Morwen, her face against the security glass in Bronzefield.

'OK, Mr Webster. Whatever you say.'

There was silence in the room.

This is for you, Morwen. They can call it the Webster Foundation in the paperwork but I'm going to make damn sure your name's right across the front of it. So people have something to remember you by.

The scent of the flowers hung over everything. Her fingers were wrapped tightly round the pen. He opened his mouth again and spoke, his voice so faint she could hardly hear the words: 'Sita'll draw up the papers. Now go. And I don't want you at my funeral.'

She didn't look back until she'd got the door open. The figure on the bed lay there, as if dead. She pushed the door to. Paul stood very close to her.

'What happened in there?' he said. 'You look different. You sure you're OK?'

'Tell you later. I'm going to get you a coat. You don't have to wear it.'

She held onto his hand, so soft and warm and vital in hers, and the young man in the nurse's uniform escorted them out of the building.

Background Note

Ardent Justice is a fantasy. Like all fairy tales it rests on truth. Tax evasion is not conducted as described here, but both tax avoidance and tax fraud are real issues and highly damaging. Estimates of the scale of the problem range from the official HMRC figure of £34bn (2015) to £150bn. The City of London is not as overtly sexist as portrayed, but gender equality in pay, promotion and prospects is still a long way off. Ministers do not conspire directly with business (so far as I know) but the amounts of tax foregone by government in recent high-profile settlements are striking.

For background on tax-dodging Nick Shaxson's *Treasure Islands* and Tony Norfield's *The City: London and the Global Power of Finance* are useful. Joris Luyendijk's *Swimming with Sharks* casts light on the world of bankers. For sexism and City culture see The Fawcett Society's *Sexism and the City: the Manifesto*, or the detailed *Financial Times* investigation in the edition for 16 June 2015.

David Kynaston's *City of London: The History* gives an overview of how the City of London developed. Finally Richard Murphy's *The Joy of Tax* considers how a simple, fair and politically acceptable tax system might be implemented, something that would have saved Ade and Paul a great deal of pain

About the Author

I'm Professor of Social Policy at the University of Kent. I enjoy hill-walking, riding my bike, holidays and looking after my grandchild (not in that order). I became interested in social policy issues after working on adventure playgrounds, teaching, claiming benefits and working in a social security office in Newcastle. I've worked in the UK, most European countries, Canada, the US, China, Korea and Japan, Australia and South Africa.

My work shows how globalised market capitalism generates inequalities between haves and have-nots and promotes a corrosive individualism that stunts our capacity for empathy, charity and love. People live for themselves and their families and vote for more privatisation and less redistribution and against a humane welfare state.

I believe that social science has many strengths in helping us understand societies in the aggregate, but often lacks an imaginative grasp of why people do what they do. We must turn to novels to gain insight into the emotions and passions that drive people's behaviour as individuals. This is what I aim for in my writing.

If you enjoyed *Ardent Justice* you might like my first novel: *The Baby Auction*, available from The Conrad Press and most bookshops and on Amazon and Google Books. Here are the first two chapters:

1

Matt was six years old and he was frightened. Mummy was holding his hand but everything was terribly wrong.

They'd gone further down the track into the forest than he'd ever been before and it was getting dark. The trees were different here, taller, packed closer together. He felt they were crowding towards him. If they got right round him he'd never find his way out.

Mummy had stopped walking. He wished she wouldn't hold his hand so tightly. They stood there, staring down the track. You could just make it out in the evening light and then it turned at the crest of a rise and you couldn't see it any more. The pine trees towered over him. He caught the smell, rich and harsh, but there was another odour he didn't recognise, with sweat and iron and something like lamp-oil in it.

He gripped Mummy's hand. She wouldn't look at him. She just stared down the track.

'When's Daddy coming? I'm hungry.'

She glanced down but she didn't smile. The sun was now touching the tops of the trees. It was night already between the trunks and the black shadows were reaching out across the track, towards them.

'Later, Matt.'

She squeezed his hand. Now she had a different look

on her face, as if she was listening out for something far away. The forest was silent; there was no wind among the trees, no bird-song. He wished she wouldn't grip his hand so hard. He felt so hungry he couldn't stand still. He wished Daddy was there and they could all go back to the village together.

He heard a rattle, like a harness being shaken hard, and the clatter of hooves on the track, then the special low whinny a horse makes when it recognises the smell of its own stable.

That's when he thought it might all be all right. He shouted:

'That's Duke!'

Duke was his favourite, the best, the most powerful horse in the village. His father always used Duke for the ploughing. Daddy sometimes lifted him up onto Duke's back. He loved the soft warmth of the horse's body. He loved burying his face in the mane and stretching his arms round the sturdy neck and feeling the great muscles move under the skin.

He let go of Mummy's hand and started to run forward. Duke rounded the corner and plunged towards him. A man, his Daddy, sat astride his back, urging him on.

'Daddy!' he shouted, 'Daddy!'

Daddy drove the horse onward, towards him. All around the great trees crowded in, the shadows black as pitch between their trunks.

He saw one of the shadows move and he felt as if his heart was being squeezed in his breast. The shadow heaved forward, separated itself from the darkness under the trees and swept out of the forest onto the track. It reared up, forming itself into a shape like a man, but black as the night between the trees. The hair rose stiff on the back of his neck.

He felt Mummy's arms round him, clasping him against her. She was trembling. Others came, men like black shadows flowing out of the forest. They made no noise. All he could hear was the pounding of hooves and Mummy screaming:

'No!'

The first figure hurled itself upward at Duke, grabbing at the bridle. It lurched sideways and was dragged along, clinging to the flank of the horse. Duke's head was wrenched round. The black shapes swarmed round, reaching up and fastening themselves onto Daddy, dragging him down.

He was on his feet, throwing his body from side to side to shake them off. Then something swept up over his head from behind and he was gone.

Matt stood there watching it all happen. His whole body quivered in horror. Then he woke up and it was dark and he was eighteen and Ed was there beside him and he loved her so much he could hardly breathe and he was telling her his dream.

2

He was standing there, right at the back of the main stand, almost against the rear wall of the City Stadium. Ed was beside him, and she had her arm tight round his waist and her head on his shoulder.

Ed's name was really Eden, but she'd told him she only wanted to be called Ed. She was eighteen too, just over a fortnight younger than him. They'd met in Re-education. She had skin the colour of cinnamon, long brown wavy hair which she often tied back, brown eyes and a smile that made Matt feel he was worth something. There was a scar the width of his thumb under her right eye, healed so close to the colour of her skin that you scarcely noticed it. That warm August day she was wearing blue jeans and a crimson tee-shirt and she was the only person out of the thousands who packed the stands who mattered to Matt.

He couldn't understand why everyone was so intent on the giant screen that dominated the stadium, on the words that kept appearing on it, all about 'Citizens' and 'Exchange' and 'The One Law'. He was more interested in the family in front of him – a couple and a boy who must have been only about six years old.

The same age I was when they came for Dad, Matt thought.

There were more people in the stadium than Matt had

ever seen in one place before. He felt uneasy. He knew that the message on the screen and the speeches of the well-dressed people he could barely make out on the platform in front of it were part of Celebration Day and that was why they were all here.

He just didn't believe any of it would make any difference. Celebration Day wouldn't help him find Mum or Dad. The parents of the small boy in front of him stood rigidly at attention, chanting the words on the screen. Matt felt his heart go out to the child, who tugged impatiently at his father's hand. He guessed from their shabby blue work-clothes and the fact that they were here, at the back, in the cheapest area, that they came from the poorest class in the city, just like him and Ed. You never got paid very much. They'd sack you if they decided they didn't want you and that meant going hungry. They were on an outing together as a family. He thought maybe that didn't happen very often.

The child tugged harder, almost swinging on his father's arm. Matt watched, the familiar ache at his heart, thinking of his own father and of his mother, of what it was like when you were a child and there was no-one who was there for you.

All he needs is a smile, he thought. *Don't ignore him. Give him a smile.* All around them the crowd were shouting

THE ONE LAW PROTECTS PROPERTY!

THE ONE LAW PROTECTS FREEDOM!

THE ONE LAW PROTECTS DIGNITY!

The noise battered at his ears. He saw the father swing round and glare down at the child. He felt the anger gathering in his chest. The man suddenly shoved the child away, so violently that he fell. Matt started forward. The child picked himself up and stared at Matt with solemn, dark eyes.

233

Matt couldn't help himself. He tapped the father on the shoulder:

'Careful with the kid,' he said. 'You'll hurt him.'

The father, thin, his narrow face prematurely lined, made to answer. Then he caught the expression in Matt's eyes, half pain, half anger, and turned abruptly away.

Matt felt a hand gripping his wrist. Ed slipped in front of him.

'The One Law protects everyone. That includes kids.'

The man grabbed his son with one hand and the woman with the other and pushed his way into the crowd. The child dragged behind, staring back at Matt, unsmiling.

Ed released Matt's wrist.

'You OK?' she said.

'Yes, I'm OK.'

He relaxed his shoulders and forced his attention back onto the ceremony. No-one paid him any attention. They were all gazing up at the screen, shouting out

THE ONE LAW!

ignoring everything else going on around them. Ed was mouthing the words on the screen beside him. He opened his own mouth in time with hers, but could say nothing, his throat constricted. Ed looked up at him:

'It's OK. Just pretend you're saying it.'

Matt never saw the point of the One Law. They taught you about it in Re-education but none of it made sense. The only good thing about Re-education was that it was where he met Ed. Matt knew he was special to Ed. Happiness tickled inside him whenever he was with her. For the first time since they'd sent him to Re-education he felt he could make something of his life.